'We have heard the [...] trate, and she fixed [...] eye which did not h[...] reports in this mat[...] attempt the Tucke[...] things for their child, and are glad to see it, but we have decided that significant harm could occur to Macaulay if he were returned home at this point. In the light of this, we make an interim care order in respect of Macaulay Tucker.'

Donna had expected it, but nonetheless gaped. Her head fell into her hands. A whimper seeped through her fingers. Dave was up and behind her, his hands on her shoulders, his lips at her ear. 'It's all right,' he murmured fiercely. 'We'll get him back, love. We'll win. Just you wait. We will win.'

Her right hand rose to grasp his. In this, at least, she realized she needed Dave like she had never needed anyone before.

Executive Producer: Ted Childs
Producer: Ann Tricklebank
Directors: Ken Hannam, Geoff Harris, Michael
Brayshaw, Paul Brown, Graham Moore, Alan Grint,
Bruce MacDonald
Writers: Peter Barwood, Jo O'Keefe, Chris Lang,
James Clare, Ann Brown

SOLDIER SOLDIER

STARTING OVER

Kit Daniel

CENTRAL

B□XTREE

First published in the UK in 1996 by
Boxtree Limited,
Broadwall House, 21 Broadwall, London, SE1 9PL

ISBN: 0 7522 0230 8

Cover design by Shoot That Tiger!

Cover photographs by John Rogers, Tony Nutley, Oliver
Upton/Carlton UK Television show Robson Green as Dave Tucker,
Jerome Flynn as Paddy Garvey, Holly Aird as Nancy Thorpe and
David Groves as Joe Farrell.

Typeset by SX Composing DTP
Printed and bound in Great Britain by
Cox & Wyman Ltd., Reading, Berkshire

A CIP catalogue entry for this book is available from the
British Library

Chapter 1

Upstairs, the officers' cheeks were almost as red as their dress uniforms. They were, at the moment, tucking into turtle soup with Madeira and a sprinkling of coriander leaves. Paddy Garvey and Dave Tucker knew that, because they had served the stuff mere minutes back, and cookie had told them so before they did it.

Cookie was a schizophrenic. Most of the time, he prepared poo stew or icky fricky with mash and duff which was spooned into tin trays. Then he was an OK sort of guy. On nights like this, however, when the Spode and the regimental silver were excavated from the vaults, and cookie was given menus which sounded like an entire staff roster of a Beirut whorehouse, he turned all Marco Pierre and strutted and snapped and swore like a proper chef. He went all artist on them.

Dave had tried the soup. He said that it was 'Knorr with haddock – a drear waste of sherry.'

Paddy, Dave and Joe were waiters this evening, but Joe was up there in the mess for this course, skulking. He had drawn the short straw this evening. He had to do glass-topping-up duties during the soup and the dessert. Dessert was the longest watch.

'End of civilization as we know it.' Dave Tucker squinted up at the glass in his hand. 'Kitchen has only one bottle of ketchup, bloody officers don't leave enough dregs to intoxicate a goldfish, and why? Because bloody officers are people like Stubbs – I mean, would you Adam and Eve it? Stubbs, an officer?' He lifted a silver cover to pinch a chip.

'So?' Paddy Garvey leaned back against the dishwasher.

'Well, we're doomed, mate. And the CO's barely out of nappies.'

'Yeah, but you're forgetting a few minor irrelevant points, aren't you?' Paddy reproved. 'Like Stubbs has only been in the army twenty years, including one year as an RSM and four years as *your* Sarn't Major, which in the eyes of most discerning persons, entitles him to a bloody medal, not just a poxy commission.'

'Oooh, best friends are we suddenly?' Dave did his best limp-wristed shrill.

'And as for Colonel Phillips,' Paddy spoke like an indulgent teacher controlling his impatience, 'He may be the youngster colonel the regiment has ever had, but he was seconded from the Royal Scots Dragoon Guards to the SAS before he had been out of Sandhurst six months, and has consequently seen more of the business end of action than we'll see in a lifetime.'

'Yeah, well . . .' Dave pursed his lips and screwed up his nose. 'That's as may be. Doesn't alter the basic facts about the ketchup, does it? Anyhow, you want to know my theory about officers?'

'Not a lot,' admitted Paddy, who could almost read Dave's mind by now.

'Exactly. Well, my theory on officers . . .' He turned as a girl clattered into the kitchen. She clattered quite seriously, as though the sound of her heels were the distinctive call of her species. She had pale skin and straight black hair. 'Hi, Colette,' Dave grinned. Colette was Joe's betrothed, or, as she would have it in her refined scouse, his 'fyongsee'. She was all right, was Col. 'Where'd you spring from, then?'

Colette rattled to the sink. Her beads supplied a counterpoint to her footfalls. She turned on the taps. 'Oh, fixing Marsha Stubbs's hair,' she said. 'Poor Marsha. She's all of a doo-dah. Her first full-dress do as an officer's wife. She's convinced she'll drink from the finger-bowl or use the wrong knife or something.'

'Stubbsie'd have to commit hari-kari, then,' said Dave. 'And good riddance, if you ask me.'

'Leave it, Dave,' Paddy sighed. He caught sight

of Joe coming down the stairs with a pile of plates. He turned to pick up a cloth. The covered plates on top of the range were hot.

'Oooh, Joe,' Colette cooed. 'I just can't wait for you to be an officer. You'll look so good in the uniform, you know.'

Joe Farrell laid down a Pisan tower of bowls. 'Oh, yeah, yeah,' he scoffed, but you could see that he was well chuffed by her faith and ambition. 'Today a waiter, tomorrow a general. One step at a time, eh, Col?'

'Yeah. Well. Excuse me,' said Dave. He waved a chip aloft. 'I was holding forth. Do I exist or what? I was about to give you the benefit of my theory on officers . . .'

Paddy liked a wind-up. 'Sorry? You say something?'

'My theory on officers . . .' boomed Dave, like a town crier, 'based on a careful study . . .'

'. . . in guard houses all over the world,' put in Paddy.

'Yeah, I thank you, Acting Sergeant Garvey.' Dave did not notice that Joe was standing to attention, nor that Paddy's face was twitching as though the same fly were repeatedly flying into his eye. 'My theory on officers . . .'

'Consists mainly on how to avoid them, I suppose,' said a quiet voice from behind him.

Dave wheeled. He gulped. He made to salute,

then realized that he had a chip in his right hand.

'So, how are the chips?' Colonel Phillips asked with just the faintest trace of a smile.

'Chips . . .' Dave looked down at the offending article as though wondering how it got there. 'Oh, beautiful, Sir.' He reached for the dish and raised the cover. He offered it. Phillips picked one carefully from the pile. 'Ketchup, Sir?'

Phillips cocked head to consider. 'Yeah. I don't mind if I do. And your name is?'

'Tucker. Fusilier Tucker, Sir.'

Paddy completed the introductions. 'Sarn't Garvey, Sir. Fusilier Farrell . . .'

'And . . . er . . . I'm Colette Daly, Sir.' Colette put on a voice which somehow managed to convey that officers were wonderful and that this particular officer looked drop-dead *gorgeous* in his finery. 'I suppose you're new here, are you?'

'Brand new.' Phillips wiped his fingers on Paddy's cloth. 'Lieutenant Colonel Phillips. Just thought I'd drop in to see how the engine room was running. Nice to meet you, lads. Colette. Oh, and thanks for the chip.' He turned with a vague little wave.

'Have a nice evening, Sir,' said Paddy after him. The whole kitchen seemed to sigh as Phillips passed through the swing doors.

'Right,' said Paddy. 'Fish.'

Donna Tucker leaned over the travel cot. She tucked in the blanket with a tenderness which might have surprised those with only a passing acquaintance with her. Donna's voice was frequently almost as loud as her clothes. Words such as 'brash' had been used of her, and even, by a certain generation, 'no better than she should be'. In general, this was merely an illusion that she gave, in large measure inadvertently. True, she was a girl who liked a good time, which was why, in the end, something had had to give in her relationship with the army, but, when it came to Macaulay, her son, Donna was as impulsive and fierce in her affection as she had been in all her other passions.

She reached into the grip for the teddy-bear and placed it at the top right-hand corner of the cot. She turned towards Macaulay, who sat on the rug in front of the television, transfixed by some grotesque Japanese cartoon. 'Here, Mac,' she said. 'Bed's all set up. You'll be good, now, won't you?'

'Ah, he'll be fine.' Sandra Quinn peered around the jamb of the kitchen-door. 'Don't you worry, Donna.'

'I forgot my toothbrush,' said Macaulay without moving his eyes from the screen.

'No, you didn't. You tried to forget your toothbrush.' Donna exchanged an amused

6

glance at Sandra. 'It's in his case.'

'Can I do you a cup of tea?' asked Sandra. She was a woman with whom you naturally associated the question. She was perhaps forty, and, with her soft, plush complexion and spumy bubbles of greying blonde hair, had plainly once been pretty, but everything about her spoke of washed-out colours, carpet-slippers and dripfeed Typhoo.

Donna looked at her watch. 'Oh, no, thanks, Sandra. I've got to be at work in twenty minutes.'

'You look very tired, loved,' Sandra purred. 'Are you sure these night shifts are a good idea?'

'Ah, we . . .' Donna pushed back a renegade hank of hair. 'It's the best chance I get to work with computers, you see.'

'Oooh.' Sandra frowned. 'But I thought it was a printing place, design, all that?'

'It is, but all that's done on computer now, you see. That's the thing about nights, you see. Copy comes in, we do the setting, the layout, the lot. Be on the streets tomorrow. But there are gaps, you know? Get a chance to do some experimenting, and I've got to learn if I'm to get anywhere.'

'Yes, well, don't kill yourself in the process, you hear?' Sandra sat on the arm of a chair and crossed calves like balustrades.

'No, no. Don't worry. I'm fine. It's only for a few months.' Again Donna looked at her watch.

She knew what the time was, but Sandra lived alone and liked to chat. She needed a reminder.

'You heard from Dave, then?'

'Er, yeah. Yeah, of course. He's coming down this weekend like every other weekend. Religiously.'

Sandra was alert to the slight sigh as Donna spoke. 'Ah, but you don't mind seeing him, do you?'

'Oh, no,' Donna was weary, but she bucked herself up. 'No, no, no. No, of course not. No, it's good for Macaulay. No, me and Dave are OK, you know? I mean he'd like more, but . . . I mean, we're still friends.' She shifted the conversation to surer ground. 'What about you and your ex, then?'

'Oh, Andy . . .' Sandra was casual. she shrugged. 'No. Not a word. What sort of fool would marry a soldier, eh?' She smiled sadly, and, to Donna's astonishment, stood and said, 'Well, I suppose you'd better be getting on your way.'

'Yeah.' Donna walked over to Macaulay. He did not look up as she bent and kissed him. 'I'll pick you up in the morning, Macaulay,' she said. She ruffled his hair as she straightened. She smiled at Sandra, mouthed, 'See you,' picked up her coat and padded to the door of the flat. She shut the door quietly. The walkway thrummed beneath her feet. The traffic from the Guildford street below sounded very loud.

Yes, she was tired, but she was going to make it on her own. If it killed her.

Sole, beef Wellington, crème brulée and cheese had been served, consumed and their debris cleared away. Now came dessert, which confused Marsha Stubbs somewhat, in that she would have referred to the crème brulée as dessert, but the menu clearly stated that dessert was yet to come. Unused cutlery and used glasses had been cleared away. Bowls of fruit and of dried fruit had been placed on the table. The regimental snuff box – a giant moufflon head set in ornate silver – had been deposited at the table's centre. Otherwise, only small conical cut glasses twinkled on the great, deep, sunset-lit lake of the table, like those lantern-festooned little junks back in Hong Kong.

Marsha suffered her tiny glass to be filled with some sweet, amber liquid. She had sipped at it, and now nervously turned the glass round and round by its stem. It was like a dog's familiar slipper. It was hers – the only thing which she could call hers in this brilliant, confusing room.

'Clockwise, Marsha . . .' Michael's whisper penetrated the burble of the voice around her. She started. She frowned. Michael was pointing at a decanter at her right side. For a moment, she could not even work out which was clockwise, then she remembered, and heaved the heavy decanter towards the Arab-whose-name-she-had-not-caught at her left. The Arab-whose-name-she-had-not-caught gave her a lingering, lascivious smile in return. His hand had brushed her thigh more often than accident could account for over the past hour or so.

And now the men were standing and giving 'The Queen', and, thereafter, chairs were pushed back, legs crossed, cigarettes and cigars were lit. Marsha would have loved a cigarette herself, but, uncertain, she sat upright, guarding her tiny glass like a sentry.

Colonel Phillips was addressing the company. He was a nice-looking chap, but still it somehow shocked her that, whilst Michael, at forty-eight, should just have been elevated to the rank of second-lieutenant, his CO should look as though he had barely left Sandhurst. But then Phillips, it seemed, knew what to do with a glass or a regimental snuff box.

'It's a great pleasure to welcome tonight our distinguished friends from Saudi Arabia and Germany, who are here for tomorrow's infantry demonstration . . .' Phillips – she must get used to thinking of him as 'Paul' – was saying.

Marsha knew about distinguished friends.

Michael had explained it all. 'We're the shop window. We can't cock up,' he had told her. 'We're trying to flog them a few million quid's worth of equipment.'

'. . . The King's Own have now been in Warminster for three months as a battle group for Combined Arms Training Centre,' Phillips went on, 'and I'm sure they'll give you a good show on the ranges. I'd love to be able to take credit for that, but, as I only arrived twenty-four hours ago, I think that might be a little bit rich.'

There was a ragged chorus of laughter, so Marsha joined in. Her laugh came out strangely high-pitched. As she sipped her drink a cough punched at her chest walls.

'So, two last things,' said Phillips, smiling, 'First, a very warm welcome to the mess to Marsha and Michael Stubbs . . .'

'Oh, God, it would have to be now that every eye turned to her, when she was flushed and doubled up and coughing into her fist. She gulped, essayed a smile as the 'Hear hears' sang in the ornate plaster coving and rattled the chandelier, then her neighbour's hand brushed her thigh once more, and another cough bubbled to her lips.

'. . . Lieutenant Stubbs has designed tomorrow's exercise and will be in overall command of the ranges . . .' Phillips continued smoothly. 'And second – me. I would like to say how honoured – and overawed – I am to take command of as great a regiment as the King's Own. So, Ladies and Gentlemen, charge your glasses please. The King's Own Fusiliers.'

Chairs scraped. Fabric sighed. The rumble of male voices made the floorboards hum.

They heard it below in the basement kitchen. Dave had to place a finger in his ear so that he could hear the voice at the other end of the line. It was hardly worth the bother, nor the twenty pence that he had so rashly paid into the telephone. 'This is Donna Deeley,' said the voice briskly, 'I'm not here. Please leave a message. Bye.'

Dave breathed a curse and slammed down the receiver. 'Deeley,' he said sourly. 'Donna bleeding Deeley.'

'Yeah, well, it's her name, isn't it?' Paddy tried to be philosophical. He had been through it all before. 'The one she was born with, I mean.'

'Yeah, yeah, I know.'

Paddy shook his head sadly. 'You've got to hang on in there, mate.' he said.

Dave winced. 'Oh, God, man. I've been hanging on in there for a year.'

'I know you have. I know you have.' Paddy's voice was a muffled drum.

Usually Dave kept up the jaunty wisecracks and the wind-ups well enough, though Paddy knew what was gnawing at him. Maybe it was a mixture of port, champagne and claret instead of Newcastle Brown and Guinness which had scoured away his inhibitions. 'I want to be with Donna and Macaulay all the time!' he objected.

'Yeah. Yeah, of course you do.' Paddy laid a heavy hand on his friend's shoulder.

'Not just a few bloody hours every second weekend . . .'

'I know,' Paddy nodded.

'Do you?' It was amazing how readily a defensive snarl sprang to Dave's lips. Paddy just gazed at him. That heavy gaze was answer enough. Paddy had been getting on with the job but had been pining for his Nancy for more than eighteen months now.

'Just . . .' Paddy licked his lips. 'Just hang on in there,' he repeated. 'All right?'

Dave blinked a bit, then nodded.

Why does a marriage break up? Silly question, really, thought Paddy as he flung off his tunic and stretched out on his bed that night. Damn it, better ask, why does a marriage take place? Every human being is so different from every other, has so many distinct fears, associations, dreams, aspirations and memories that the whole idea of two lives in tandem is downright absurd. Things change. People grow at different rates and in different ways. Eighteen-year-old girls make vows of celibacy before they even know what it is to be twenty-six and broody. Sixteen-year-old boys commit themselves to the army before they even know what it is to be raunchy, adult, independent. Those contracts are unconscionable, so how in God's name can a woman and a man – already from foreign countries by reason of gender – vow that, for the rest of their lives, they will run in harness in the same direction and at the same speed for the rest of their days?

Paddy could not blame Nancy for leaving – well, yes, he could blame Nancy, and sometimes, in his cups, had called her many vile names, tasting with relish the foul savour of the words - but, when he was calm, like this, when sadness rather than anger coloured his thoughts, he was prepared to acknowledge that he too, had he been in her position, would have found it hard to do other than she had done.

That, of course, was the problem with loving the person who hurt you. You could not hide in contempt or hatred.

Nancy had started her work as a redcap with his encouragement. She was too bright simply to be another Army wife on the eternal treadmill from gym to supermarket to coffee morning. The trouble was, he had never reckoned on her being good at the job – so good that she was offered a place on a sergeant's course and was tipped for a commission. It was not that he resented her success or even her seniority. It was just that, although she knew that it must mean separate postings, separate lives, she was nonetheless not prepared to turn the opportunity down. 'And why the hell should she?' Paddy murmured to himself. After all, there was no reason why she should be held back by her husband's steady but unremarkable career. He would never have considered being held back by hers.

Paddy had tormented himself through many months, because he could not bring himself to say – or even to approve – what he felt. He wanted a wife waiting at home for him. Soldiering was hard and often lonely. He needed a companion, a helpmeet, and yet he knew that he would sooner have a feisty, competent, amusing woman like Nancy than a whole harem of hausfraus.

So Nancy had gone, and Paddy had fretted and lain awake like this night after night. Oh, there had been other girls, but they had always and only been substitutes. Try as he might to shake thoughts of Nancy from his head, he felt her absence like that of an amputated limb, and he could not in fairness to those other girls permit them to think otherwise.

As for Dave and Donna, they were soulmates. Their married life had been made up of endless rows and equally passionate reunions. Both had played away from time to time, but both were too similar and too fair-spirited to bear grudges. Donna had not left Dave so much as left the Army. The restrictions imposed by life in married quarters were too much for one accustomed to instant gratification and with a weakness for a pretty face, and Dave, for all his carping and moaning, loved the Army and his comrades. He doted on Macaulay, but was no Lothario, no uxorious speech-maker. When things went wrong, he was happier to tell a joke and to crack a can with the lads that to buy flowers or shell out for the candlelit tête-a-tête. He did not realize until it was too late that there were soft-spoken Lancelots out there, all too willing to flatter his improbable Guinevere.

So Donna too had gone. Paddy had seen other separations, other divorces, but they were usually the culminations of years of dislike. Dave and Paddy were peculiarly unlucky. They were those rarities: men who still loved their estranged spouses, but did not know what to say or do to win them back again.

If Colette clattered, Donna jingled. Together, they would sound like a troika on a stage. Donna had bangles around her wrists, earrings which hung as low as a basset hound's ears, and further chains about her waist. She was shedding her coat even as she entered the studio. She puffed out cold air and breathed in hot. She wove her way between tables to her own. She flung her coat over the back of her chair and sat. Almost at once, her fingers started flicking over the keys of the computer console.

'You're late,' The lean, dark, hook-nosed Mrs Roach appeared at Donna's side like a genie. She spoke without rancour. 'Where've you been, for heaven's sake?'

'Sorry.' Donna chewed gum. Her fingers kept moving. 'Dropping my kid off at the minders, then waiting for a bloody bus.'

'Hm . . .' Mrs Roach held out a sheaf of papers. 'Well, since you're here . . . This boxed ad. The Dance Academy. That's Times. I marked it Opal. Why have you changed it?'

Donna shrugged. 'I tried Opal. It looked a bit naff, I thought. Opposite the Baskerville there, I mean.'

'Oh, right. Ah, I see.' Mrs Roach sniffed. 'You've been here - what? Six months? - and you know better than the person who designed this?' She did not wait for an answer. 'Well, as it happens, you're absolutely right. I'll tell them we're changing it.' She spared Donna a thin smile. 'Good girl,' she said, 'You're doing fine, Donna . . . Even if you do say that my designs are naff.'

Donna grinned happily. That 'good girl' meant more to her than a thousand of those meaningless compliments which she used to value from no-hopers wanting to get in her knickers. This was a tribute that she had earned.

If she had had a tail, she's have wagged it.

Chapter 2

The visiting dignitaries, who now included a junior defence minister, sat in tiered seats overlooking the valley. Clouds hung low in the sky above, and there was an edge to the breeze which spoke of coming rain.

Michael Stubbs tried the microphone. The feedback squealed, so he gave it up as a bad job. He shouted above the breeze instead. 'Welcome to Warminster Range, Gentlemen. On Range C . . .' he pointed, '. . . we have four platoon commanded by Lieutenant Forsythe. They will now demonstrate the taking of a trench system in open country. We will be using live ammunition with flanking fire from two general purpose machine guns.'

Down on Range C, Jeremy Forsythe gave his usual chirpy grin and signalled to Paddy Garvey. 'Very well, Sarn't Garvey!' he gave a mock salute. 'Carry on.'

It was all that he needed to say. The King's Own had been working on the Warminster Ranges day in, day out, honing their skills with weapons, vehicles, tactics, signals – the works.

Paddy had known long periods of bookwork in his army career, long periods, too, of training for specific environments or of developing specific skills, intermingled with periods of actual soldiering, but never before had he worked so long or so hard with a single body of men to create a homogeneous assault team.

Joe Farrell was already prone at the machine gun down at the right. Dave Tucker was manning the mortar which would soften the target up before the APCs went in. Two woomphs, two spurts of dust from the trench as the shells blew, and the platoon moved forward.

All hell broke loose.

Up there, the small arms fired and the big tank guns boomed. Back here, the mighty machine guns gave blistering covering fire. Suddenly Paddy noticed a break in the rhythm. He turned to where Joe Farrell lay wreathed in smoke and dust. Joe was wincing, gritting his teeth. Dave Tucker was struggling with the magazine. Jeremy Forsythe was there too, shouting into the field radio.

Paddy crouched low and scampered over. He flung himself down. 'What's up?' he yelled.

'Jamming!' Dave shouted succinctly back.

Stubbs's twanging Yorkshire voice came over Forsythe's RT. 'Hello, Bravo Zero Alpha. Send sit-rep, over.'

'Hello, Zero,' Forsythe called back. 'This is Bravo One Zero Alpha. Number Two gun jamming. Have ordered cease-fire. Over.'

'Zero,' Stubbs's voice stabbed, 'Maintain full support-fire. Over.'

Forsythe looked grim. He sighed. 'Bravo One Zero Alpha,' he insisted, 'Strongly recommend not to. Gun constantly jamming. Over.'

Paddy could hear the bullish bloody-mindedness in Stubbs's voice. 'Zero, we want both guns. I say again, *both* guns. Over.'

Forsythe exchange a glance of frustration with Paddy. He spoke through lips tight as a razorshell. 'Bravo One Zero Alpha,' he spat, 'Roger. Out.' He laid down the RT and nodded to Joe. There was a moment's silence in that emplacement. Dave seemed to be cursing, but made no sound. All three men eyed the gun and cringed from it as Joe once more put his shoulder to the stock, lowered his eye to the backsight and curled his finger around the trigger.

Paddy was four feet away, but he felt the shockwave. Somewhere in all the noise and the black cordite smoke, Joe squealed. 'Oh, shit!' Paddy and Dave both reached for him. As the smoke cleared, they saw him reaching out blindly, his face black and bleeding.

Forsythe was already on the RT. His anger made his voice shake. 'Hello, Zero, this is Bravo

Zero Alpha. Breech explosion. One casualty. Over.'

Paddy was standing up. He bawled. 'Arms down!'

The RT crackled. Stubbs asked, 'Zero, do you require casevac?'

'Bravo One Zero Alpha, yes!' yapped Forsythe. 'Immediately. Over.'

He turned his attention to Joe, who lay groaning and sobbing on the turf. Dave was already kneeling over him, soothing him as his fingers explored the injuries.

'I can't see! God! I can't see!' Joe moaned.

'Easy, now,' Dave crooned. 'You're all right. Stay still, breathe deep. Don't worry. You're all right, pal.'

'Yeah, hold on.' Forsythe reached into his pack and pulled out the Verey pistol. A flare wailed as it spurted through the watery air. On the RT, Stubbs was announcing, 'Hello, all stations. End Ex! End ex! End ex!'

There was sudden silence, then came the familiar judder of a helicopter, distant at first, then louder and louder. The downland grass bowed low like breeze-blown flames as the chopper descended. Paddy, Dave and Forsythe crouched low over Joe's writhing body.'

The orderlies had jumped from the chopper before it had touched the ground. They rolled Joe quickly and carefully onto the stretcher. They raised it and trotted back to the chopper. 'Hang in there, Joe!' Dave shouted after them, 'You're going to be all right!' Then again the men had to crouch as the rotors wagged faster and faster and the chopper arose into the cloudy sky.

'Will he be all right, Tucker?' asked Forsythe as the sound once more diminished.

'Reckon so, Sir.' Dave wiped blood and soot on his trousers. 'Dunno what damage has been done to the retinas, but otherwise it's just flesh wounds and shock.' He looked up at where the spectators sat. 'No bloody thanks . . .'

'Thank you, Tucker,' Forsythe interrupted smoothly. 'That will be all.'

'Yes, Sir,' said Dave. He noted with approval that the lieutenant's eyes were also flashing with anger. 'Wor Jeremy' was a public-school sort, and therefore a toffee-nosed prat, but as toffee-nosed prats went, he was not bad, and 'not bad', in Dave's books, was high praise indeed. Dave guessed that Stubbs was not going to walk away from this fiasco without trouble, and that was all that concerned Dave.

'Macaulay?' Sandra Quinn tied a headscarf as she bustled into her living room. She was irritated and impatient this morning. She had not had much sleep last night. She sighed when she saw Macaulay still sitting on the rug staring at *Thomas the Tank Engine*. 'Macaulay, come on. I told you to get your boots and coat on. I've got to get some money from the post office.' Macaulay made a sullen little move, but did not turn away from an adventure which, according to Ringo's droned commentary, concerned Gordon and Terence. 'I'll buy you an ice cream, Mac . . .' Sandra tried cajolery. It did not move him. 'Look, I can't leave you here on your own. Come along. I've got to have that money for eleven. I promised the rep I would have it . . .' Macaulay sat still and stared ahead.

Sandra took a deep breath. She sighed through gritted teeth. 'All right, all right,' she said as though he had come up with a persuasive argument. 'All right, you can stay here.' She slung her handbag over her arm. 'Look, I don't want you to move from here, right?'

Macaulay sat still and stared ahead. His eyes seemed glazed. They reflected the movements of the trains on the screen.

'And I'm going to ask Thomas the train to look after you, OK?' She walked to the door. 'I'll only be a few minutes, right? And you stay right there, you hear?'

Macaulay sat still and stared ahead. Only when the door had shut again and he heard her footfalls on the walkway did he quietly and scornfully whisper, 'It's Thomas the *Tank-Engine*, actually.'

Only now too did he show signs of animation. He got to his feet and walked through to the kitchen. He pulled open the fridge door. He frowned, then looked about him. He caught sight of the milk bottle up on the formica-topped work surface. He had to stand on tiptoe to reach it, and even then, he could not close his fingers about it but had to push it along with his fingertips. It was coming closer . . . closer . . .

Suddenly it put on a spurt towards the edge. It hit the rim and toppled. He tried to catch it, but his hands were too small. The bottle shattered, splashing a bright star of white on the brown vinyl. Macaulay crouched as it fell. He reached out as though to put the milk and the glass back together again. A jagged shard of glass punctured his skin. He yelped. Blood stained the milk pint. Angry now, he struck out at the glass as though to punish it. Again pain sprang up his arm. Again blood splashed on to the floor. He keened and sank to the floor. Then he studied the damage. The sight hurt more than the sensation. He took a good deep lungful of air, and wailed.

There was no response, so he gave it a bit more wellie, and this time drummed his heels on the floor. He fell back on to his back and tried to bore a hole in the ceiling with his shrieking.

It was four or five minutes before a dumpy little figure in a skirt appeared at the frosted glass door. The bell rang. A frail voice called 'Sandra? Sandra?' Macaulay howled.

It was another minute before the little, crumpled face appeared at the kitchen window. Then running footfalls drummed.

It was a full ten minutes more before a siren drowned out Macaulay's plaints. More running feet came up the stairs. The glass of the door was shattered. A dark-blue arm hooked in to turn the latch.

Macaulay was in safe hands.

Dave Tucker need not have worried. Stubbs was very rapidly realizing that he was in for a deal more trouble than he had bargained for. Colonel Phillips attempted to make light of the incident in front of the visitors. 'Well, Gentlemen,' he announced, 'I'm afraid that our demonstration has proved slightly more realistic than we intended. I suggest that you follow our Sergeant Horan to Range D where the exercise will continue. I will join you as soon as I can . . .' He smiled, but, as he turned away and strode towards Stubbs, there was thunder in his glare.

And then it got worse.

A sandy little chap in MP's uniform stepped

into Phillips's path. Stubbs's heart sank still further.

'Sarn't Major Fellner, Sir,' the MP saluted.

'Sergeant Major,' Phillips courteously returned the salute. 'I didn't know we had the military police here.'

'Special Investigations Branch, Sir. Could you tell me what happened, please?'

'I know very little at present,' Phillips admitted. 'Merely that there was a breech explosion on the machine gun.'

'Yes, Sir,' Stubbs heard the man snap, 'I'm afraid SIB will have to investigate this.'

Stubbs stepped forward, jaw set. 'Are you suggesting that range discipline wasn't up to scratch?' he demanded.

Fellner looked surprised at the interruption. 'No, Sir,' he said patiently, 'But we've had a number of similar incidents in the past few months. So . . .' he turned back to Phillips, '. . .if you don't mind, Sir?'

'Of course we will give our full co-operation.' Phillips fixed Stubbs with his glare. 'But right now, you will appreciate that I have an injured man, and he must be my first priority. Thank you.' He caught sight of Forsythe leading his platoon back. 'Ah, Forsythe,' he called, 'take your platoon back to base if you please. I want the MO's report on Farrell a.s.a.p.'

Stubbs saw the expression on Forsythe's face. It was, if anything, still more damning that the CO's frown. Stubbs's cheeks sprouted deep crimson flowers. 'Sir . . .' he started.

'Mr Stubbs,' Phillips was brusque to the point of dismissiveness, 'let's get on with the work, shall we?' He marched fast past him. Stubbs had no choice but meekly to follow.

'Thanks, love. You must be beat,' Mrs Roach smiled up at Donna. 'I'll make sure you get a good whack. I mean, we could have told them to stuff their new front page, but it's part of the job, you know. I'd never have got the bloody thing to bed on my own.' She drank coffee and shuddered. She looked up again with heavy-hooded eyes. 'You get on home and have a good kip.'

'Huh.' Donna mustered a smile and a shrug. She drained the tenth mug of black coffee of the night. She laid the mug down on Mrs Roach's desk with a hand which barely trembled. 'Some bloody hope with Mac about. Best chance I've got, shove him in front of *Fireman Sam* or something, catnap for a few minutes at a time. It's just I feel so guilty. I mean, you don't want your child growing up with square eyes, do you?'

'I think what he'll need most is a mum who's *compos mentis*. Use the video, Donna.'

'Yeah.' Donna shrugged on her coat. 'You're

right. Well, I'll be off, then. See you Friday.'

The telephone shrilled at Mrs Roach's elbow. 'Yup. See you Friday. And thanks again for all your help.'

Donna shouldered her bag and walked a little unsteadily to the office door. Once on the landing, she pressed the button to call the lift. Usually she used the stairs for the sake of the exercise, but she wasn't sure that she could cope with them this morning. She had been gazing at a VDU since seven-thirty last night. It was now half past eleven in the morning. The whole world wobbled as though reality was an amateur holiday video.

The lift hummed. The bell pinged. The doors opened like jaws. Donna stepped in, pressed the button marked 'G' and leaned back against the wall. She closed her eyes.

'Donna!' The office door puffed. Mrs Roach's footfalls rang in the stairwell. 'Telephone! Donna . . .!'

The doors were shutting. Donna reached for the bank of buttons again. The doors slid reluctantly open. 'What . . .?' Donna stepped out on to the landing. 'Who is it?'

'Woman called Sandra. Got her knickers all in a twist. On line two . . .'

She pushed open the office door. Donna breathed, 'Oh, my God . . .' She was suddenly very wide awake, and wished that she were not.

She ran for the telephone and snatched it up. Mrs Roach watched as Donna said, 'Hello? Sandra? What . . .? You – you left him? Oh, Jesus Christ, is he all right? Where is he? What . . .? Oh, God . . .' The colour had drained from Donna's face. 'Yes . . . Yes, see you there.'

She laid down the receiver and reeled. She raised a hand to her forehead.

'What is it, Donna?' said Mrs Roach softly.

'It's Mac. He's . . . She left him on his own. He cut himself. He's . . .'

'Where is he?'

'At . . .' Donna gulped and stared. 'At the hospital.'

Mrs Roach had her keys out. 'The General?'

'Yes.'

'Come on. I'll drive you there.'

'What?' Donna was in shock.

'Come on, Donna,' Mrs Roach grabbed her elbow and pushed firmly. 'We're on our way.'

Sergeant Nancy Thorpe looked up as Fellner marched back into the office. She grinned proudly. 'Hi, Sir. Just heard. The Donaldson case. Guilty on all charges. Breaking and entering, assault and battery, GBH. Bingo, basically.'

'Good, good.' Fellner laid his cap and gloves on the desk. 'Right, well, I've got another one for you.'

'Something juicy?'

'Nope. 'Fraid not. Breech explosion on the ranges this morning, that's all. Sarn't Larkin will be looking after the gun and the ammo. I want you to look at the men. See if there's negligence.'

'Right.' Nancy picked up a pen and clicked it. 'What's the unit?'

'Er . . . King's Own Fusiliers.'

Nancy's pen checked above the paper. The tip of her tongue emerged at the corner of her mouth. She sighed. 'Oh, well, I suppose it was inevitable at some stage, especially being stationed here in Warminster.' She wrote.

'Hmmm?' Fellner was looking at some papers. 'Sorry? What's inevitable?'

'The King's Own,' Nancy nodded slowly. 'It's my ex-husband's regiment.'

'Ah . . .' Fellner considered. 'Yes. Right. What's his name?'

'Garvey,' Nancy briskly snapped her notebook shut. 'Paddy Garvey.'

Fellner found the name on his list. 'Sergeant Paddy Garvey. Hmm. You be all right?'

'Don't worry, Sir,' Nancy grinned. 'I'll be fine. Really.'

And in truth, for all that she dreaded what was to come, she could not wait to get started.

Donna barged through the swing doors of the

hospital. She scurried across the bright yellow foyer to the reception desk. She told the girl behind it, 'Hello, I'm Donna Deeley . . . Donna Tucker, I mean. You've got my son Macaulay. I . . . Is he OK?'

The girl did not so much as look up. She droned. 'Someone'll see you shortly, Mrs . . .?'

'Tucker.'

'Mrs Tucker. Yes, so, if you'd like to sit down . . .'

'But have you . . .' Donna burbled, 'I mean, you haven't even looked. Macaulay Tucker. I mean, at least if you know where he is, who's been treating him.'

'We are all very busy, Mrs Tucker,' the girl's voice seemed to slouch. 'I have your name and will make contact with the appropriate ward as soon as I have time. Now please just sit down.'

Donna flounced to a moulded plastic chair and sat down hard. She glowered at the receptionist, which, considering that the receptionist did not look up from her romantic novel or whatever else she was reading behind the desk, was pretty pointless, but it made Donna feel better.

After five minutes, Donna decided to stand and pace. She marched back and forth past the reception desk for a further five minutes or so, punctuating her parade with muttering and sighs. At last, an auburn-haired woman in a powder-blue twinset and sensible brown shoes entered the room and padded directly across the foyer to Donna. 'Mrs Tucker?' she cooed, 'I'm Dawn Rawnsley.'

'Yes.' Donna nodded. 'Yes. Sorry. I've come about Macaulay. I believe – Sandra told me that he – he cut himself, is that right? Is he all right? Can I see him?'

'Yes, yes, he's fine now. He's been seen by the doctor and he's fine.'

'Oh, thank God.' Thus reassured, Donna turned to anger. 'I just can't believe she left him by himself,' she seethed. 'Can I see him, then? Sorry.' she winced. 'Sorry, aren't you the . . . Aren't you the doctor?'

'No, no. Come along with me, Mrs Tucker. We'll get this sorted out.'

Donna followed the woman down one green-painted corridor, then turned left into another. She was ushered into a room lined with filing cabinets. Two other people were already in there. Neither of them was Macaulay. The man with the iron-grey and flashing bifocals had 'doctor' written all over him. The woman with the dark bun and the big bust was also of a distinct and familiar type. Her posture was almost military. Her eyes were blank as marbles. There was a smug, complacent set to her mouth. Her chin was held high. She looked vulnerable.

'This is Mrs Tucker,' announced Mrs Rawnsley. She shut the door. Donna suddenly felt strangely confined. She turned round. She frowned. She looked first at the strange man, then to the woman, then, as if for consolation, to Dawn Rawnsley.

'Er, Doctor Gerie,' the powder-blue woman indicated the man, 'and WPC Stainton from the Child Protection Unit. Please have a seat, Mrs Tucker.'

Donna glanced around the room. She sat reluctantly, but this Rawnsley woman had a way of making requests sound like orders. 'What's going on? Donna demanded. 'He is here, isn't he? Why can't I see him?'

'Mrs Tucker,' intoned the doctor in a voice from the tomb, 'I examined your son at the request of Social Service. He had a bad cut to his right hand . . .'

'Yes. Yes, I know. Sandra Quinn told me. You want to talk to her about that. Leaving him alone. I mean, of all the irresponsible, criminal things to do . . .'

'The cut itself is not serious,' Dr Gerie continued like a talking textbook, 'but I noticed that Macaulay was experiencing some difficulty with his right ear. When I examined him further, I found severe bruising above the hairline and inflammation of the ear drum. The bruising is consistent with a heavy blow to the side of the head. A blow from an adult hand.'

Fury seemed to heat Donna's veins even as terror chilled them. Someone had hit Macaulay. She would tear whoever it was apart. At the same time, she saw the way that these people were looking at her. They were not three separate people. They were one blank wall of official disapproval and stubbornness.

'Are you trying to say . . ..?' Donna squeaked, 'Are you saying as someone's hit him?'

The wall remained silent. She looked from one to the other component in search of a single sympathetic or human response, in search, even, of a flicker of doubt. 'Well, why don't you tell me?' she demanded, 'Is he all right?'

'He is now,' said Dr Gerie. 'Yes.' He nodded as he spoke. God damn it, both women nodded in unison.

'Well, where is he?' Donna yapped. 'I need to see him. Now.'

'Mrs Tucker,' said the policewoman gravely, 'Can you in any way explain these injuries?'

'No . . .' Donna stared. 'No, of course not. Have you asked Macaulay?'

'We have spoken to Macaulay, yes.' All three of them were nodding again. How could 'we' talk to a child? 'He seemed frightened. He won't say anything.'

'Well, then, it must be Sandra Quinn!' Donna shrugged as if it were self-evident to any right-minded person. 'Have you asked her?'

'Mrs Quinn is an approved childminder,' enunciated Dawn Rawnsley in her best Julie Andrews voice. 'There has never been any previous complaint about her.'

Donna looked at the three certain faces. She said softly, 'Oh, no. No. No. Oh, no. No way. I have never hit my kid. Are you saying . . .? Never! Never, you hear? She was the one left him alone. Approved childminder? Why don't you talk to her?'

'We have talked to Mrs Quinn,' said the policewoman. 'She said that she was worried about you and Macaulay. You were working too hard, under a lot of pressure, she said, living on your own, doing double shifts all the time. She says you were very tired and a bit snappy with the child.'

Donna went on the offensive. She pointed. 'Are you accusing me? Are you? You listen to that lying cow and not to me? Look, I've had enough of this. I'm not standing for this. I want my kid back. And now!'

Dawn Rawnsley had obviously learned her quiet, rational voice from a school. It did not sooth. In fact, it irritated the hell out of Donna. 'I'm afraid that there can be no question of our allowing him back into your care at the moment.'

Donna was up and out of her seat, eyes blazing. She lurched against a filing-cabinet, then against the wall. She trembled. 'Crap!' she shrieked. 'You give my kid back or I'll bloody sue you, you hear? You can't do this! He's my kid! You give him back or I'll finish you, all of you! He's my kid!'

The Rawnsley woman patted down the air. 'I am very sorry, Mrs Tucker, but we have direct responsibility for Macaulay's safety . . .'

'And I haven't?' Donna sobbed.

'. . . and, as there is no explanation for his injuries, we cannot agree to give him back into your care,' continued the woman smoothly. Christ, she was a walking bloody sub-section. Did she have blood in her? *Did she have children?* The question rang like the shriek of a lathe of steel in Donna's skull. What was happening here? How in God's name was this possible?

'We will therefore be applying to the Family Proceedings Court immediately for an Emergency Protection Order which will place Macaulay under our care . . .'

'No! No!' Donna shook her head. A child could not live with a 'we'. A child – a Macaulay – needed human beings with faults and affections and passions. He needed his mam and his dad.

Donna drew a deep breath which came out like a donkey honk. 'You can't do this . . .' she sobbed, and she meant it. They could not do this because there was a law, a government, a Queen. They could not do this because Nature too had laws.

'I am afraid that we can. And we believe we must.' There it was again. 'We can . . .' 'We believe . . .' How could you fight with a 'we'? How could a 'we' have feelings? 'However, it is the court that must make the final decision, and you should consult a solicitor immediately so that he can advise you of your rights.'

'No . . .?' Donna's fingers scrabbled uselessly at her leggings for want of a throat. Somewhere in this building was a little boy with smooth dark hair and a brilliant, wicked smile, a confused and lonely little boy who needed his mother's arms about him. Donna shook her head fast. 'No, no, no. No, wait. I've done nothing wrong! I'm not leaving here without my child! This is wrong! This is . . .' Suddenly all assertiveness fled. Her voice came from deep, deep within her, a low moan of pure pain. 'I've got to see him. I've got to . . .'

'As soon as we've obtained the order, we will arrange for you to see him at a foster home.'

Foster home? Foster home? Someone else would take charge of him? Someone else put him to bed, read him stories, wake him up in the mornings? No. Donna flew at the woman. 'Nooo!' she yelled, and her hands reached out like talons to strip this official mask from what should be a human face. 'You can't do this! You can't! I've done nothing wrong! He's my child! He's my Macaulay.' She found herself checked by the strong grip of the policewoman. Her knees sagged. 'He's mine,' she drooled, 'You can't.' She sank to her knees, her mouth open in a silent scream.

'Mrs Tucker,' said the policewoman, 'Please don't make things worse for yourself.'

All three of them escorted her to the door of the hospital and left her on the steps before returning to the smug warmth of their office. Donna was left out in the cold to return to a home which was no longer a home.

Chapter 3

Phillips found Jeremy Forsythe bent over the snooker-table in the Officer's Mess. He said, 'Jeremy, hi. I wanted to catch up with you earlier, but these punters demand a great deal of their salesmen. What's the latest on Farrell, then?'

'He's bearing up, Sir,' Forsythe potted a sitter of a red. The cue ball bounced back off two cushions to end up in baulk. Forsythe grimaced as he straightened. 'There doesn't seem to be any serious damage, but they're keeping him in overnight for fear of concussion, you know.'

'Hmmm,' Phillips sipped his whisky. 'Well, I'll go and see him tomorrow. So,' he said slowly, 'why did it happen, Jeremy?'

'Sir?'

'The breech explosion. Come on, Jeremy.'

Forsythe shrugged. 'I think it was an accident, Sir.'

'Yeah,' Phillips nodded without conviction. 'Well, we'll find out soon enough, won't we? Look, while I've got you here, Jeremy, there is one more thing.'

'Sir?'

'The position of Second in Command, B Company.'

'Uh, oh.'

'Yup. Look, we've got a tough schedule ahead of us over the next few months, including an overseas exercise, possibly in Australia. Now look. You're the obvious candidate, but I have to say that at the moment, you'd be a lot more useful in the field with your men. I don't want to take anything away from anyone else, and I'm not soft-soaping you, but they know and respect you – even the old hands.'

'Yes, thank you, Sir.' Forsythe's disappointment was palpable. He sniffed. 'Er – can I ask who is getting the job, Sir?'

'Temporarily, Lieutenant Stubbs.' Phillips seemed to feel that an explanation was called for. 'Look, it's an administrative role, Jeremy, and Michael's had experience organizing these overseas junkets many times.'

'Yes, Sir.' Forsythe could see the sense in the decision, but it saddened him all the same. He had often heard of typists who were too good at their jobs and so remained in the typing pool whilst others, less able, prospered. He worried lest he might suffer the same fate.

He was not a man given to bitterness, and, had it not been for a couple of brandies too many, had it not been, too, for the fact that Michael Stubbs lounged on a sofa with a defiant, almost proprietorial look on his face, almost as though he had been the paterfamilias of the mess instead of a bloody Johnny-Come-Lately, Jeremy might have passed him without a word. As it was, he flung himself down on the sofa and said casually, 'Congratulations, Lieutenant Stubbs. Second on Command, B Company. Well done.'

Stubbs pursed his lips to stop himself smirking – or, at least, that was the uncharitable interpretation that Forsythe put upon the expression. 'Thanks very much.'

'Good work on the ranges today, too. One man injured, of course . . .' Forsythe slapped his thigh and waved away such trivia. 'But what does that matter as long as you're making your mark, eh?'

Stubbs bridled. That jaw shifted forward. 'Meaning?'

'I told you quite clearly that that gun was jamming.'

Stubbs breathed deeply and noisily through his nose. 'Ah, go to bed, lad,' he sneered.

Forsythe was on his feet. 'Don't patronize me!' he snapped. He was aware that he reeled slightly, aware that he was in the wrong – at least as far as mess protocol was concerned, but the anger had been festering inside him since this morning.

'Well, grow up, then.' Stubbs raised his eyebrows. His smile was small and thin. It is of such things that great wars are made.

It was Forsythe's turn to breathe deeply until the scraps of scarlet had cleared from his view. He slammed down his glass and turned on his heel. It was the best that he could managed just then.

Colette crept into the hospital room for fear that Joe might be sleeping and, if she was honest, because she wanted to see his face, to come to terms with it, before he could see her expression. He was watching television, so she had a split second in which to sigh in relief. He was still her Joe. Yes, he had bandages wrapped around his crown and a few dash and asterisk black wounds around his eyes and on his cheeks, but they would mend. He turned to face her.

'How are you?' she purred.

He shrugged. 'Itchy.'

She perched on the edge of the bed. 'The doctor – I talked to her on the way in. She's nice.'

'Yeah?'

'Yeah. She says you're going to be all right.'

'Yeah. Yeah, sure. Just have a face like a butcher's block is all.'

'You won't.' She laid a tentative hand on his thigh. 'Anyway, according to the doctor, you won't.'

'That matters to you, does it?' He was sullen.

'Yeah. Course it does!' Colette breathed. 'Joe? What's wrong?'

'What's wrong?' Joe swallowed. He was all choked up. 'Well, could it be the fact that I get visits from four of me mates and me bloody platoon commander before my fiancée bothers to turn up?'

'I didn't know, Joe!' Colette protested quietly. 'I was out of the office all afternoon. I didn't get home until eight. I came as soon as I found out!'

Joe was not heeding her. Shock had shaken him. 'I mean, if it was you – if you were in trouble, I'd do anything. I'd ... I'd shoot me mates and me platoon commander, but I'd be there. Oh, yeah, but it's different for business-woman of the year, Colette Daly, isn't it?'

'I – did – not – know.' Colette spelled it out in monosyllables. She had recognized the self pity of a lost child. She smiled as she reproved him. 'My name's not Doris Stokes, you know. I mean, I didn't happen to have my crystal ball with me at the time.' Her eyes danced as they looked into his. His filled with tears. She drew him to her.

'Oh, Col!' He shook. He closed his eyes and pressed hard against her breast. The tears seeped slow and heavy from between his eyelids. 'Jesus, I was scared, Col! I was scared! I thought for a moment that . . . that I'd lost everything! I'd lost you! So I'm lying here thinking, what's holding me to you, eh? A ring I haven't paid for. It's not much, is it?'

'It's enough for me.' She stroked the hair at his crown. 'What else do you want?'

Joe shook his head as though to burrow a hole in which he could take refuge. 'I don't even know where . . . what you think, or feel! I just want to know where I stand, Col.'

She gently pulled his head back. She bent and kissed his lips. It was one of those kisses like a pebble thrown in a pool. It started small and central, then spread, rippling wider and wider until large waves lapped at the outer edges. It was altogether a pleasant and overwhelming experience, and Joe was letting himself drift in the reassuring luxury of it all, but suddenly Colette had pulled herself out of his arms and he was once more alone and colder than ever.

He opened his eyes and he frowned. 'Colette?' he groaned. 'What are you doing? Come back!'

She turned on her way to the door. She raised a finger to her lips. 'Shh!'

'What are you doing? Colette! Come back!' He was grinning now. It hurt.

Colette pushed the door shut with a click. She reached up to switch off the light. 'You know what you want do,' she whispered. He heard her shoes clatter as she kicked them off, then her stockinged feet padded on the lino floor. There was a hiss of fabric, a hot breath of air, then suddenly the blankets were plucked away and her weight was on him, her hair falling upon his face, her lips slithering on his. He reached down to find warm naked flesh where she had rucked up her skirt.

'There now,' she giggled in a deep, throaty voice. She hissed as she sank into him.

'Colette!' he wrenched his mouth from her. 'Not here!'

'Shh!' she said again. She held his face between her hands. She started to move on him.

'Mmm,' he groaned. 'God! Nurse!'

'Shut it,' she ordered, and they laughed into one another's mouths.

Jeremy Forsythe was the first witness whom Nancy interviewed. She was not complaining. He had joined the King's Own after the regiments had amalgamated and Nancy's contact with the regiment had – well – dissolved. She took readily to his glossy good looks, his gleaming smile, his precise but easy manner.

'Steady, Nancy, girl,' she told herself – not for the first time in such circumstances. She remembered the young Captain to whom she had similarly warmed until it was proved that he had beaten up not just his wife but a string of prostitutes into the bargain.

'No,' Forsythe was saying, 'When it jammed a third time, I ordered the gunner to cease fire.'

'So why did he start again, Sir?'

Forsythe sighed. Nancy recognized the smoked-glass screen which had slammed shut across the young officer's frank face. You got used to that. Corps loyalty was highly prized in the Army, which made SIB's job doubly difficult. 'I got an order to recommence firing,' Forsythe said at last.

'And who was that from?' Nancy did not look up from her notebook.

'The range officer, Lieutenant Stubbs.'

'Did you inform him that the gun was jamming?'

'Yes.'

'Did you agree with his order?'

'He was in charge of the exercise. It was not for me to agree or disagree.'

Now Nancy looked up from under frowning eyebrows. 'Let me rephrase that question. Did you protest the order?'

'I pointed out that the gun was jamming,' said Forsythe stubbornly. 'Look, it was an accident. There's nothing anyone could have done about it.'

'Except, I suppose, not gone on firing the

machine gun, as you advised?' Nancy permitted herself the luxury of a small smile.

Forsythe gave a little shrug but said nothing.

'Thank you, Mr Forsythe,' Nancy turned a page with finality. 'If you would be so kind as to ask Mr Stubbs to step in . . .?'

Where Forsythe marched out with respectful formality, Stubbs swaggered in, gazed out of the window, turned to see Nancy and, as though surprised, said, 'Ah, yes. Can I help?'

'I hope so,' Nancy said. 'Please sit down, Mr Stubbs.'

Stubbs considered for a moment, then pulled out the chair and sat on it, leaning back with his legs set wide.

'You are aware of the nature of our investigation, Mr Stubbs?'

'Yes. You're looking into the breech explosion on the ranges - why, I must say, I cannot think, unless you think someone booby-trapped the gun.'

'Because,' Nancy said calmly, 'we are profoundly concerned about the safety of military personnel. As, I am sure, you are. Now, the sequence of events seems clear enough. Lieutenant Forsythe had informed you that the gun had already jammed three times, is that right?'

'No!' Stubbs protested, then, more calmly,

'No, I didn't know how many times it had jammed. No.'

'But you did know that it was jamming?' Nancy took Stubbs's sulky silence for assent. 'Did he advise that the gun should not continue firing?'

'He . . . er . . .' Stubbs sighed, but his tone was still that of one who considered that such matters were no concern of a chit of a girl. 'Yes. All right, he did.'

'But you gave the order to continue firing nothwithstanding?'

Stubbs leaned forward on the desk. He explained as if to an idiot. 'Listen, sweetheart. It was a big day, right? There were a lot of top brass there. Savvy?'

'And that, to your mind, constituted justification for risking the blinding of one of your men?'

'Don't be . . .' Stubbs thought better of it. 'No, of course not. Ridiculous. It was a decision made at short notice in the field, that's all. You wouldn't understand.'

Nancy made much of turning pages to check. 'Mr Stubbs,' she said at last, 'I note that you were very recently commissioned. Was this exercise your first command as an officer?'

That got to him. 'What are you saying?' he spat.

'Nothing, Sir,' Nancy was all innocence. 'I am

just trying to establish what happened – and whether it was avoidable.'

Stubbs made a noise like a puncture. 'Right,' he muttered. He stood and strode to the door. He pulled it open.

Again Nancy kept her eyes on the papers before her. She spoke very calmly. No buggers called her 'sweetheart' and patronized her. 'Er, could you close the door, please?' she said politely. 'I haven't quite finished with you yet . . .'

Stubbs hesitated, It suddenly dawned on him that, for all his seniority, this little bit of a girl held his career in the palm of her hand. He growled and sighed deeply, but he shut the door and returned to his chair.

Donna had found the solicitor through Yellow Pages. She had picked upon this particular practice because of the attractive layout and the typeface chosen for the big boxed ad, but discovered on enquiry that neither Messrs Isherwood, Jones or Partridge, the gentlemen featured in the ad, would be available at short notice, but that one Mr Kurtah, a junior who was 'very good at Family' would meet her at midday today.

She had spent the past half hour, then, sitting in this musty office, explaining her circumstances to this impossibly youthful and scruffy young man, and now he put down the telephone to tell her. 'Yes. Sorry about that. Now, Social Services have been granted the EPO as I expected. The Emergency Protection Order basically means that they keep your boy with foster carers until the hearing, which is set for next Tuesday. Then a magistrate will decide whether Macaulay remains in care or not. So we'd better get our acts together, right?'

'Yeah,' Donna nodded. She frowned. She could not think exactly what she should do.

'Now, what about your husband?' Kurtah was all enthusiasm, like some overgrown puppy. 'Do you still see him?'

'Yeah . . .' Donna was hesitant. 'Yeah. Sure, twice a month.'

'Aha. Right. Have you told him?'

'Oh, God!' Donna's right hand flew to her mouth. 'He's coming to see Macaulay tomorrow.'

'So, how long have you been separated?'

'Er . . .' Donna was transfixed by the young man's pen, as though it might steal the words from her. 'About a year.'

'Friends?'

'Yeah, I suppose . . .' Donna shuffled forward in her seat to correct any false impressions. 'Look, Dave hasn't got anything to do with all this. I look after Macaulay, and I'm going to get him back.'

'Look.' Kurtah slapped down his pen. He stood. He ran his fingers back through his abundant hair. 'I have to be honest, Mrs Tucker. This isn't looking good . . .' There was no window in here, so he scanned a tall bookcase instead. 'Social Services' main concern is Macaulay's safety. They will argue that you are living on your own, that you are working hard and that you're under too much stress to manage the child properly. Therefore, so the story goes, he's still at risk while he stays with you.'

'But that's . . . That's crap!' Donna whined. 'I've done nothing wrong. I look after Macaulay, and when I'm not with him, I pay for a childminder!'

'Sure, sure. You know that and so do I.' Kurtah leaned over her and crooned. 'But we're left with the inexplicable, inescapable fact that someone – we don't know who – has abused your child. That is our problem. That's what we've got to face.'

'So . . . so what are you saying? What do I do?'

Kurtah did something that she had never seen anyone save actors playings Sherlock Holmes do before. He flung himself back in his oak swivel chair and placed his fingertips together beneath his lower lip. 'Mrs Tucker, is your marriage really so broken down that you and your husband couldn't get together for the child's sake?

Show the court that Macaulay is more important to you than whatever differences you may have had in the past. I have to advise you that that is your very best chance.'

Donna was saying 'No,' before he was halfway through his speech. She continued to say it as though continued repetition might drive away the very idea. 'No, no, no. No! I've done nothing wrong. I'm fighting this on my own. No. No. No.'

Kurtah studied her. He nodded slowly. A long, deep, clogged sound seeped from his lips. He raised his eyebrows. 'Very well,' he said. 'We'll do our best.'

Colette turned up at the hospital at ten past one. She had left early for her lunch hour and urged the taxi-driver all the way as if she had been a weary horse. She need not have bothered. She found Joe happy and smiling today.

He reached up to kiss her. 'Well, they're letting us out at four, and they're giving us a week's convalescence.'

'Hey, that's great!' Colette bounced on the bed. 'I'll get some time off too, then.'

'Great.'

Colette laughed. 'You should get yourself blown up more often.'

'Oh, thanks. Sure.'

'Now, listen.' Colette took Joe's hand. 'Before I forget to ask you, there's something I want us to do together.'

'Mmm?' Joe was cocky after last night's performance. 'Sounds promising.'

'No, silly,' she hit his arm. 'No, not that. Not just that.' She kissed him lightly. 'Listen. Did I ever tell you about us and Kenny McGann?'

Joe frowned. 'Kenny . . . No.'

'Only won the silver medal at the Birkenhead Roxy for our tango when I was sixteen.'

Joe snorted. 'You never? Well, I'm not surprised you kept that one a secret.'

Colette looked hurt. She said, 'Oh.' She gazed down at his hand and separated the fingers, one by one. 'Well, I started again, Joe. Dancing. Ballroom dancing.'

Joe considered her. His lips twitched to one side. He said, 'No.'

'You and me . . .?' Colette pleaded.

'No!'

'And me sequinned bolero. Crushed velvet . . .'

'No!'

'Oh, please, Joe.' She held both his hands now. 'Please. We never do anything together any more.'

'Yeah, we do,' Joe pouted.

'Oh, yeah, I forgot.' Colette flung down his hands to fold her arms. 'Yeah, I forgot. We get up, go to work, have breakfast, have a drink. I mean nothing different! Nothing adventurous . . . sort of.'

'Fine, so let's do something different, then. OK. Fine, but I'm not bloody dancing!'

There was silence. Colette hunched her shoulders and breathed. Crossly. Joe rolled his eyes heavenward and muttered a silent prayer.

'Anyway, listen,' he said at last. 'I've been thinking. . .'

'Careful. Don't want you having a relapse.'

'Oh, ha ha. No, it's just . . . I been thinking of what I said yesterday. I sort of – well, came at it the wrong way.'

A smile just tugged at the corner of her mouth. 'Felt fine where I was sitting.'

He laid a hand on her shoulder and lightly squeezed. 'No. What I wanted to say was, you're the best thing that I've got . . .'

'Yeah, I know.' She checked herself and giggled. 'Sorry. Only kidding. No. Go on.'

'. . . and that's why I want to marry you. That's why I want to start a family.'

She turned back to him. She took his hands once more. She leaned towards him and laid her cheek against his. 'Joe, I love you, but I don't think I'm ready to start a family yet, and I'm . . . I'm certainly not ready to marry into the Army. I just – I just don't want to get stuck in a rut.'

'Oh.' It was a sad, dull little sound. Joe's shoulders sank. 'Well, will you just think about it, please?'

'Yeah,' she whispered in his ear. 'Yeah, OK. I'll think about it.'

'Col?'

'Hmm?'

'Were you serious about this dancing thing?'

'Nah. It's all right. Forget it. It doesn't matter.' Colette sighed and nestled in there. She could not see the look on Joe's face, which turned from resignation to tenderness to sudden, fierce determination.

Paddy Garvey presented himself at the desk in the anteroom of the MP prefab prompt at 1400 hours, as ordered. 'Sarn't Garvey come to see Sarn't Major Fellner,' he announced.

The young man at the desk had a colourless crewcut that put Paddy in mind of a vole. His face was very thin and gaunt. He bared prominent canines. 'Certainly. One moment,' he said.

He led Paddy down a narrow corridor and knocked on a red door at his right. A woman's voice called, 'Yes?'

The rodent-man put his head through the door. 'Sarn't Garvey, Ma'am,' he twanged. His vowels were strangely flat.

'Thank you,' said the woman's voice. Paddy

frowned. The rodent-man stepped backward into the corridor. Paddy strode into the room. And stopped.

'My my, Sarn't Major Fellner,' Paddy croaked, 'How you've changed.'

Nancy stood at her desk. She had the grace to look a little shy. 'He couldn't make it,' she said.

'Oh.' Paddy shuffled. 'Well, what a pity.'

Nancy walked round the desk and they stood like dancers waiting for the first chord. 'I did try to get out of this,' Nancy told her shoes.

'Out of interviewing me? Yeah, well, thanks very much.'

'Paddy . . .'

Paddy's chin went up. 'Sarn't Garvey to you, I think, Sarn't Garvey.'

'Sergeant Thorpe, actually.'

'Oh, yeah.' Paddy spoke softly. 'Of course. Yeah. You managed to wipe out all traces, didn't you?'

She shook her head hard. 'It wasn't like that,' she said.

'No.' Paddy relented. He sighed. 'No, I know it wasn't like that. I'm sorry. It's OK.' He tried to smile. 'I mean, I'm choked, but it's OK.' He looked down at the beret in his hands. 'Well, how've you been, Nance?'

'Oh . . .' she flapped a hand. She returned to her seat behind the desk. 'Getting along, you know?'

'Getting along very nicely by the looks of it.'
Paddy sat opposite her. 'So, you miss me?'

'Yeah, every minute.' She looked up and her
eyes sparkled with mischief. 'What's your name
again?'

Paddy smiled. That was the Nancy he remembered, and, God, how he wished that it was not,
that she had somehow turned into someone
dumpy and humourless and hideous. But no.
This was still Nancy, and she was still throat-
clutchingly lovely.

'Right. Now business.' Nancy noisily cleared
her throat. 'You know what I'm investigating.'

Paddy winced. 'You know, I still can't believe
this. I had no idea you were here.'

'Yeah, well, I was.' Nancy caught Paddy's gaze
and turned away as though burned. 'Er, now . . .
Right. You are 44597623 Sergeant Paddy
Garvey, King's Own Fusiliers, First Battalion.'

'That's very good,' Paddy smiled.

She looked up again. 'I – I heard about your
Queen's Gallantry Medal, by the way. I was
really proud of you.'

'Been following my career with interest, have
you?'

'No.' She turned back to the refuge of her
papers. 'Now, yes, the breech explosion. Could
you tell me what happened?'

Paddy waited until she looked up. He was not

going to make this easy for her. 'Perhaps you could tell me what happened.'

'On the range, Sergeant Garvey. Did you hear Mr Forsythe advise Mr Stubbs not to continue firing?'

Paddy crossed one leg over the other. He clasped his ankle. 'God, I have missed you, Nance. You know that?'

Nancy did her best to glare. 'Look, I could delay this interview until Sergeant Major Fellner is available,' she warned.

'No, no.' Paddy held up his hands, palms outward, as though to halt the traffic of her words. 'No, I'll behave. OK. Right, what did you want to know?'

'About Mr Forsythe.'

'Ah, yes. Right. Er . . . Well, I think a bit of background information might be useful first.'

Nancy frowned. 'Background?'

'Yes. Yes, starting in Hong Kong two years ago.'

'*Paddy*!' she squealed, not for the first time in her life, but this time she could not contain her exasperated frown.

'Nancy?' said Paddy, all innocence.

'Grrr,' she said.

The following morning, Joe Farrell rang the bell of Michael Stubb's new house in a leafy suburb of Warminster. As he waited on the doorstep, Joe appraised the sort of house that he and Colette could hope for if ever he made it to officer status. Not bad, he thought. Certainly a lot better than Joe had ever known in his upbringing. Double garage, so a man could do a bit of carpentry or welding in his spare time; nice little garden at the front, bigger, private lawn of which he had caught a glimpse round the back. What? Three, four bedrooms? Plenty of room for the children for whom Joe longed. Yeah, you could just imagine it: Lieutenant – no, Captain Farrell and Mrs Farrell and their three children. Colette with – what? A sporty little Mazda or Vauxhall, doing the school run, while Captain Farrell climbed into his MG . . .

'Joe! How nice to see you. Are you OK? I heard about the accident.' Joe was jolted back to the present to see Marsha standing in the doorway.

'Er, fine.' Joe's head swivelled to left and right. 'Look, Marsha. I'm not here, right?'

'You're not here.' Marsha smiled sympathetically.

'As far as Colette is concerned. She mustn't know.'

'Ah,' said Marsha, as if she understood absolutely. 'So why are you here?'

'Listen, Marsha, can you dance?'

Marsha cocked her head and frowned. This strange man seemed about to ask her to bop on the front lawn.

'No . . .' Joe was struggling. 'No, I mean, really dance. You know, ballroom stuff – tangos, waltzes, the Fred and Ginger thingy.'

Marsha's face still had not entirely cleared, but she was approaching comprehension. 'Well, I know the basic steps, but . . .'

Joe sighed as though all his problems were solved. 'Oh, great. Look, can you teach me?'

'Teach you?'

'Yeah, like, give me lessons, you know?'

'Oh, Joe, I can't.' Marsha laid an elegant hand on his sleeve. 'You know I'm an officer's wife now.'

'Yeah, yeah,' Joe gulped, 'but I don't know anyone else. And we needn't tell anyone. And Colette did do your hair, didn't she?'

'Oh, very sly, Joe,' Marsha reproved, 'But – sorry – why on earth do you want to learn ballroom dancing?'

'Oh,' said Joe simply, 'to get her to marry me.'

At last understanding dawned. 'Ah,' said Marsha, and a fond, sympathetic expression softened her features. Romance was something that Marsha could always understand. 'Weeell . . .' she considered.

'Please, Marsha . . .' he pleaded.

It was Marsha's turn to glance up and down the street. 'You'd better come in, Joe,' she said, and stepped quickly backward.

Chapter 4

Donna was at the door almost as soon as the bell stopped ringing. She said, 'Hi,' and turned away from Dave so that he would not see the redness and puffiness about her eyes. She had not dared to call him, had told herself that it would be easier face to face, but now that he was here, she was having serious second thoughts.

It shocked her that Dave must be used to such curt greetings, for he said nothing in expression of reproof or dismay, but merely followed her in. He peered into the living room, then, before she could stop him, strolled into Macaulay's bedroom. 'Where is he?' Dave called, sing-song. 'Do I know where he is? I think I do.' He bent to peer under the bed. 'There he . . . isn't.' He straightened with a frown. 'I've got him a certain toy that he likes . . .'

He smiled again. He glanced in the bathroom, then came through to the kitchen at the end of the corridor. Donna was bent double, one hand on a work surface, the other clutching her stomach. She said, 'Dave . . .'

The smile was wiped from Dave's face as if it

had been a smear on a glass. 'Where is he? Donna?'

Donna tried to speak, but it came out as a frail little squeak.

'Donna?' Dave was beside her in two rapid strides. 'Donna, what's going on here?'

'They've taken him away!' Donna blurted. 'Social Services . . . They've taken him into care! They think . . . They say . . . I hit him!'

She heaved a huge honking breath, then sobs attacked her from within, pummelling at her lungs and shaking her frame until she had to slide forward on to the kitchen table.

'What?' Dave snapped down at her. 'You hit him?'

'No!' she wailed, 'No, of course not!'

'Who's hit him?' Dave was searching for an enemy, 'Who's hit him?' He grabbed her shoulder and pulled her up. 'And where were you?'

'He – he was with his childminder!' Donna hiccoughed. 'She left him on his own and the – the police found him, and . . .'

'The police?' Dave still propped her up. A lot of men had seen Dave Tucker in fighting mood. None had seen him looking as dangerous as this. 'And where were you?'

'I was at work!' she groaned as though she had just confessed to adultery with a Hell's Angels' chapter.

'Oh, so you were at work,' Dave sneered. He let her drop on to the table-top again. 'What? Your precious job? Your bleeding design course? What happened this time, then? Your boss good-looking, was he? Or has your precious Mark shown up again?'

'That's not fair!' Donna was begging. 'Yes, I was delayed by extra work, but I rang to say so, and she was a registered childminder! I love Macaulay! I've looked after him. He means . . . he means the world to me!'

'Yeah?' Dave shouted above her sobbing. 'Where is he, then? He means the world to you, Donna, where is he? Eh?'

'I don't know,' she moaned, 'But it wasn't me, Dave. It wasn't me! You've got to believe us! I love him too much. I love him more than *any-thing*! I would never, ever do anything to hurt him.'

Dave was looking for something to smash, but he suddenly stopped his frenzied, twitching movements. He breathed deeply for a couple of minutes whilst Donna still shook and sobbed. He turned. He said, 'No. I know you wouldn't.'

She raised her face all stained and streaked and gleaming. She said, 'I'm so sorry, Dave!'

He nodded. He held out his arms. He said, 'All right, love. Come here.'

'Oh, Dave!' she whimpered, and she ran for

the warmth and shelter of his embrace as if towards death after torture.

They saw Macaulay that afternoon, only he was not Macaulay – not the Macaulay that they knew. His foster mother, Mrs Edwards, was nice – so nice, even to these horrible, violent Tuckers who spoke common and who beat up their child – that she made Donna's teeth ache. And that wasn't fair, of course. The woman genuinely was good and kind, but here amidst all this bloody niceness – the nice, full-length brocade curtains, the freshly upholstered sofa, the matching garden and lawns, the nice flower arrangements, the nice faded pictures of English cottage gardens, the nice fat yellow Labrador, all in a dinky detached doll's house in a suburban avenue, backing on to a nice common, it was all too much for Donna. It was all too much for Macaulay, too. He was confused all ends up, and, not knowing how to cope with his confusion or to express it, hid in sulky silence. Sulk long enough, and things usually got sorted.

Only Dave seemed able to cope with it all. He just sauntered in as if he'd been living in such places all his life, winked at Mrs Edwards and gave her one of those boyish smiles, then strolled into the living room where Mac sat on the carpet, surrounded by toys. He was gazing at the television again. He understood what happened in there.

'Hi, Mac,' said Dave, just as if they'd been at home, 'Brought you something.' He thrust a large black Power Ranger at the boy.

Macaulay looked up briefly. He said, 'I've got that one.'

Mrs Edwards squirmed a bit in the doorway. 'I – er – I gave him some of my kid's stuff,' she said apologetically.

Dave shrugged. He sat on the rug beside Macaulay and watched the television as though it were the most interesting thing that he had ever seen.

Donna had held back, terrified of making too much of an emotional big deal of the reunion. Dave had warned her against that, and she knew that he was right. Her distress could only confuse Macaulay further, yet she had not trusted herself to see his eyes and not to grab him, press him to her, hug him till he squeaked. Now she took her cue from Dave. She sat on Mac's other side, let her hand lie flat on the rug in such a way that the warmth of his back was against her arm. She said, 'Hi, chuck.' She too watched the box. Dave's hand was on hers now. It felt right.

'Are we going home now?' asked Mac.

'Ah, not yet, mate,' Dave smiled. 'You know your dad. Always off on adventures, sorting the world out. This time, I need Mum's help, but we'll get it sorted soon enough, eh, love?'

Her eyes met his. They were oily and wide and agonized. They said 'Yes, Dave. Yes, *please.*'

'Table for two?' asked the waitress in the tweeny's frills.

'Er, yes, please,' Marsha gave her best duchess's smile. 'Lovely'

'Oi,' said Joe as he followed her nervously between the tables. He eyed the dance floor, where the shuffling of nine or ten couples nigh on drowned out the strains of *Charmaine* from the Palm Court Quintet in the corner. 'I mean, you do remember how to do this, don't you? I mean, our Col was Birkenhead under-fifteens Rumba and Latin American Champion.'

'Yeah, well,' Marsha flapped her damask napkin as she sat. 'My speciality was more the fake tan. Now, let's order the eclairs and the Earl Grey, then we'll give it a go.'

Joe kept looking around him. He leaned forward to confide. 'I think everyone's looking at me.'

'Well, no wonder,' Marsha was enjoying this. 'You look like you've come off worse in a fight with a cheese-grater.'

Ten minutes later, Marsha had dragged him out onto the floor and was studiously ordering the movements of Joe's feet. 'That's it . . .' she said, then, 'Ouch!', then, 'Head high, proud, imperious, and . . .' then, 'God knows what my husband would say if he could see us. That's it! Good!' then, 'No, no . . . Joe, are you sure this is going to work?'

Another ten minutes later, a tall, lean man with a white moustache took pity on Marsha. He tapped her on the shoulder. 'Excuse me, Ma'am. Mind if I cut in?'

Marsha grinned as she deferred. She returned gratefully to her table and her eclair while the old gentleman took Joe in charge. 'Now, lead with the right,' he ordered in stentorian parade-ground tones. 'Hand in the small of my back. That's it. Splendid. Er, I'm Squadron Leader Barnes, by the way . . . and turn! Retired.'

Joe's cheeks were red-hot. 'I'm Fusilier Joe Farrell,' he murmured. 'Active.'

'Ah,' woofed Barnes. 'Splendid. Thought you were the military type. Point that toe now, and . . .'

Marsha luxuriantly wiped cream from the corner of her lips. As Joe swung round to face her, she grinned broadly and waved. Joe gritted his teeth, and concentrated on dancing.

Knights of old just had to fight dragons for their loves, not do the bossa nova with them.

Those were the days.

It was Marsha's day to be a refuge of sinners, it seemed. She returned home in the dusk to find a familiar figure jiggling on her doorstep. At first, as she parked the car, she refused to believe the evidence of her eyes, then she told herself that there could not exist two people of the same shape and stature who affected such clothes and such earrings. But what in God's name was Donna Tucker doing down here in Wiltshire? Oh, they had kept in touch. Donna had sent long lettercards adorned with flowers in which she wrote of her work and of Macaulay's development. Marsha had replied a little more circumspectly, but then, Marsha generally had less news to report, fewer adventures to recount.

Until now, it seemed.

'Donna?' Marsha squinted into the shadows of the doorway. 'Heavens, it is! Donna! How nice to see you! What are you doing here? Come on in. Come on in.'

Donna sighed deeply as she walked into the hall. The door shut behind her. She was grateful for Marsha's welcome, grateful for her maternal smile, grateful at last to be in a place which spoke of warmth and comfort. A home. Yes, of course, Mrs Edward's joint had been a home, but a home in which she had no place. Here at last she felt that she might put her feet up, acknowledge her grief, talk unguardedly.

'Something,' said Marsha as she walked past her, 'is badly wrong. Right?' She bustled ahead into the living room. She switched on lamps, then the flickering gas fire. 'Sit down, kick off the shoes, have a cup of tea or a drink and tell me what's up. You look dead on your feet.'

'Oh, God,' Donna moaned. She did as she was instructed, 'I wish I were.'

'Right. Which is it? Tea or drink?'

'Drink, please, Marsha, love. I've had enough tea to float a bloody battleship. Vodka tonic if you've got it. I haven't dared touch a drink these past few days for fear they'd breathalyse me for breathing with excess alcohol in my blood.'

'Who's they, and what's going on?' Marsha quickly poured the drink. 'I'll get ice if you want it . . .?'

'Nah. Forget it.' Donna reached out for the glass. She sipped and sighed. 'Oh, that's good. OK. Listen, sorry to turn up on you like this, but I tried phoning and you weren't in, and it was sort of a last minute decision to come down here. I couldn't stay up there on my own, and Dave said, "why not come down with us? Just for the evening? At least you've got mates down here." And . . . Oh, God, Marsha, I'm in a hell of a fix.'

Marsha sat on the sofa and halted the flow. 'OK,' she said. 'Unwind. Tell me what the problem is.'

Donna told her.

'Hold it,' Marsha told her when the tentative trickle of words had once more risen to a flood. 'Hold it, so the solicitor says you should get back with Dave, right?'

'Yeah.' Donna wiped a tear away with her sleeve. 'He said I'd stand a better chance of getting Macaulay back. At the hearing, like. More stable background, that sort of stuff.'

'Well, yes,' Marsha nodded, 'I can see that.'

'Yeah, but it's not fair, Marsha!' The tears once more burst from Donna's eyes. 'I mean, everything – everything was going fine. I was making it work, you know? I mean, thousands of women work and bring up children on their own, so why can't I?'

'Yes,' said Marsha hesitantly, 'but if it means getting Macaulay back, surely that's all that matters, isn't it?'

'Yes, but it's not fair on Dave!' Donna persisted, 'I wouldn't be going back because of him!'

'No. You'd be going back because of Mac, but Dave would understand that.'

'Yeah, but . . .' Donna floundered. She flapped her arms as though drowning. 'We're all set up in Reading, you know? I mean, I've worked hard, I'm getting somewhere in my job. I've got a flat. I've got a whole life! And it's nothing to do with the soddin' Army. This means – this

72

means getting sucked back in, and I'VE DONE NOTHING WRONG!' This last statement had been made so often in the past two days that it had become the title to Donna's song. It emerged in upper case.

'Donna, listen.' Marsha was suddenly firm. 'You get Macaulay back and worry about all that stuff later. You hear? Otherwise, I can tell you, you're just going to tear yourself apart.'

Donna stared at her, wide-eyed, as though the parish priest had just sworn at her. She started, very slightly, very slowly, to nod. Somewhere out there behind her, the front door opened. The wind bounded in. The door banged shut again.

'Well?' whispered Marsha urgently.

Donna sniffed and gazed up at the ceiling. 'Yeah. Yeah. OK.' she announced.

Michael Stubbs swaggered into the room. He took in the sight of the two women sitting so close together, face to face. He said, 'Aye aye . . .' and brusquely marched through to the kitchen. He returned a moment later with a can of Coke. 'Not interrupting anything, am I?'

'No,' said Marsha grimly.

Donna was already collecting her things. 'No. No, I'll be off.'

'OK, love.' Marsha stood. 'I'll see you out.'

At the front door, Marsha just touched

Donna's shoulder. She said, 'Good luck,' then retreated into the hall. She shut the door and turned. She was ready for the fray.

She was not disappointed. 'Is she having an affair with you now?' Michael greeted her from in front of the fireplace.

'Oh, don't be so bloody pathetic, Michael!' Marsha scoffed.

'Listen, sweetheart,' Stubbs pointed a finger. 'You are now an officer's wife, and you have got to be a whole lot more careful about who you mix with. Do you understand?'

Marsha sighed. She said simply, 'Donna is my friend, Michael.'

Stubbs did that irritating little thing with his head as though he had just caught an unpleasant scent on the breeze. 'I don't give a toss,' he announced.

'Yeah, well, I do give a toss.' Marsha spoke with insulting patience. 'She's just had her child taken away from her, and you stroll in and treat her like she's a bloody squaddie. Well, she's not. And I wouldn't like to see you treat a squaddie like that, come to that. Not off duty. She's my friend. And she will be my friend even if you are a pigging general.'

Stubbs opened his mouth as though to say something, then closed it again and strode from the room.

This dignity bit wasn't as easy as he'd thought.

Paddy Garvey walked past the white house three times before pushing open the gate and shambling up the garden path. There were lights on in the windows. They just dabbed the enravelment of rose tentacles which surrounded the porch. There was music in there too – some sort of cool, sparse jazz in which instruments bickered in short statements. He had not known that that was Nancy's kind of music.

He could not find a bell, so he raised the brass knocker and brought it down twice. The music became momentarily louder. Footfalls approached. Paddy adopted a relaxed and only mildly heroic stance. A small, teasing smile played on his lips.

The door swung inward.

A tall, slender man with swept back hair, an open-necked shirt, baggy cords and pale suede shoes said, 'Hi.'

The man smiled, but, as far as Paddy was concerned, the smile was of the sort which said nothing save, 'You should try my dentist.'

'Hi,' said Paddy, trying to sound chirpy.

The man raised his eyebrows. He was a good-looking sort of guy if you liked the old-style cigarette-ad type. Tailor's block in tweeds. That sort of thing. 'Can I help you?'

'Er . . . Yeah. I'm sorry.' Paddy looked upward as though perhaps the house were a tower block in disguise. 'Does Nancy Thorpe live here?'

'Yeah.' The man turned his head to call over his shoulder, 'Nance! Someone to see you!'

Paddy's heart sank. Nancy emerged in the hall in slippers, jeans and a loose sort of shirt that might have been consigned to Sue Ryder by Hamlet. 'Oh,' she said. 'Um, Paddy, this is Nick. Nick, this is my ex-husband.'

'Of course!' the man called Nick held out a frank, honest hand and smiled a frank, honest smile. 'I thought I recognized you. I've seen photographs.'

'Oh,' said Paddy, knowing that women did not exhibit photographs of their ex-husbands on mantelpieces but showed them in giggly demonstrations of albums. 'Oh, really?'

'Yeah.' Nick's arm encircled Nancy's shoulders. She did not flinch, but neither did she lean back. 'So, d'ye want to come in for a beer or something?'

'No.' Paddy's smile was anything but frank. 'No, thanks. No, I'm fine. I was just – just passing.'

He was aware as he spoke how absurd it sounded, considering that he was toting a bottle of wine and a bunch of flowers, but it would have to do.

'Yeah. I was just passing. And . . .' he gave a jokey, circular wave, 'now I'm going.'

He backed off down the path, 'Bye, then. Sorry to bother you . . .'

Nick had retired back into the house. Nancy was for a second visible through the narrow crack in the doorway. Her voice was very small as she said, 'Bye, Paddy.' Then the door swung shut.

Warminster station does not have a busy social life. It has not even the occasional thrill of having a big noise from the cities pass through with a disdainful hoot. A few times a day, it is visited by small, modest trains from Bath or Westbury, all of which arrive, stop for a while and quietly back out again.

Dave saw Donna down to the day's last such train. It would take her back to Westbury, where a larger, louder relation would take over the responsibility to get her to Reading. It was drizzling now, and the rain swept in successive veils across the track and through the puddles of light on the platform.

'So because it looks like it's the only way I'm going to get him back . . .' The cold wind whirled around them as they walked past the waiting room. Donna shivered.

'We're going to get him back,' corrected Dave.

'OK, we're going to get him back, I'll . . .' she paused and turned to him. 'I'll live with you again, if that's all right with you.'

Dave grinned and punched his palm. He breathed, 'Yes!'

'Yeah, I'll move back here.' Donna tried to curb his enthusiasm. 'But you must understand, Dave. I'll be doing it for him, not for you.'

'Yes. Yes, I know.'

'And . . . and things won't be like what they were. I mean, I - I still need to go my own way. Can you handle that?'

'Hey, Donna.' Dave held out his hands as though someone had just asked if his *gelati* were really Italian. 'Listen, I love you, OK? Nothing's changed. Not for me. But I love him too, and if I never saw either of you again, I'd much rather he was with you than with some stranger. Got it?'

Donna nodded dumbly. She tried to say, 'Thanks, Dave,' but the words would not come. The whistle shrilled. She turned and clambered up into the train. Dave shut the door behind her.

'Don't worry, love,' he called up to her. 'We'll get him back.'

She nodded and turned away. It had been a long, long day.

Chapter 5

Donna had never realized quite how naked you felt in a court of law. Not only did these people – all of them confident in their own environment and treating human weaknesses and agonies as all in a day's work – have the right, as it seemed, to enumerate your every private failing; they also had the right to accuse, both falsely and, on occasion, truthfully, without your having a concomitant right to stand up and deny the accusations, or, at least, to qualify them. She wanted to stand up and scream, 'Life is not like this!' and, 'Has none of you, in exceptional circumstances, behaved like an idiot? Has none of you had a drink too many and sung a rowdy song in a bar or thought that you were in love because you were pining for affection, or had a blazing row because you had a headache?'

I mean, listen to this pompous jerk Lidgate, who claimed to be acting on Macaulay's behalf but plainly thought that he was Perry Mason. 'Social Services contacted the regimental families' office. They were told that your marriage was far from stable . . .'

Then Dave was on his feet – looking handsome in his one suit and tie. An absurd old joke popped into Donna's head. 'What do you call a Geordie in a suit?' 'The defendant.' Yeah, well, she saw the truth of it today.

'What?' Dave was protesting. 'They said that? Listen, what are you talking about? Please let me . . .'

Yah. Let me *explain*. Sure, we had our screaming matches, sure, we called one another every vile thing we could think of at the time, but that was just our way. It was just who we were. We never hurt anyone, did we?

But the magistrate was telling Dave to shut up. 'Mr Tucker,' he was sighing, 'you will speak when I ask you to . . .'

Lidgate looked smug. 'They were also told that your husband had a serious disciplinary record, including violent offences . . .'

Yes! OK! So Dave's a hothead! He's been in a few fights. but 'violent offences' means, like, picking on someone weaker than you, mugging, murder . . . What sort of mealy-mouthed idiot calls a fight between consenting adults 'violence' and a few rows 'an unstable marriage'?

'. . . And that there had been infidelities on both sides . . .'

What? A few little slips is all. A few temptations when they were miles apart, yielded to and

80

as rapidly regretted. These people – judges, MPs, that sort – they were too important and serious to have a few small infidelities. Oh, no. They ran off with their bleeding secretaries, abandoned their families and called it love!

Ah, at last. At last, Kurtah was on his feet. 'Madam,' he said, 'Just how is this relevant?'

Exactly. Donna nodded. What had any of this to do with whether Dave and she loved Macaulay and cared for him? They were human. That was all. And surely Macaulay was better off with humans for parents than ageing bloodless Kens and Barbies like this crowd.

The magistrate looked down at Lidgate through her gold-framed bifocals. 'Yes. Exactly what is your point, Mr Lidgate?'

Well, hooray for her. Donna rapidly reassessed this woman, who plainly understood that a child's bond with its parents far outweighed any trifling sins.

Lidgate was unembarrassed. 'I am trying to establish why the Tuckers separated, Ma-am. And why we should believe that the reasons for that separation have now suddenly disappeared.'

The magistrate's lips twitched once, but she nodded. Lidgate was turning back to Donna. 'Mrs Tucker, you say that you are returning to your husband in order to supply a stable home for your son. Can I ask just when you reached this decision?'

Donna squirmed. 'Well, er, I guess it was two days ago . . .'

'Ah, so this reconciliation was very quickly and conveniently arranged?'

'No!' Donna winced, then, 'Well, we got our kid taken away from us, and we thought . . . Well, one of the things they're saying, only it's not true, is I'm too tired to do the job properly. If there are two of us . . .'

'Yes, yes . . .' Lidgate interrupted. 'Now we come to this potentially serious injury . . .'

Dave Tucker closed his eyes and gazed upward. He said, 'Oh, God, please don't take him away . . .' and his voice ended on a little whiplash squeak. Donna reached across and took his hand. When Dave at last looked at her, his eyes were full of tears.

Colonel Phillips was giving a punch bag a serious sorting out. He stripped better than his lissom outline in uniform might suggest. His shoulders were broad and strong, his chest deep, his stomach a switchback of ridges and afforested dingles. Stubbs was fit, but, as a spectator, found himself identifying with the bag.

'Hello, Sir.' Stubbs headed for the bench press.

'Ah, Michael.' Phillips reached out to restrain

his sparring partner. He panted. Stubbs noticed the sweat that wriggled down his left shoulder. 'Good.' Phillips wiped his mouth on the boxing glove. 'I was hoping to catch up with you. I spoke to Fellner – you know, the SIB man. Have you had any thoughts about that breech explosion at all?'

Stubbs sighed. He turned over his hands and studied his palms as though his life lines might tell him the answers. 'To be honest, Sir, I haven't thought about much else. Fact is, Sir, I should have listened to Lieutenant Forsythe. We didn't need both guns.'

'You mean you could have avoided the explosion?'

Stubbs nodded wearily. 'Aye. I think so. And I'm very sorry, Sir. It was a big mistake.'

Phillips sauntered across him. 'Well, I'm glad you said that, Michael, because that was also the conclusion of the SIB investigation – in which, to make matters worse, you were a singularly unco-operative witness. That was the conclusion, I say – the unofficial conclusion. Officially, you are completely exonerated. The technical officer's report showed that the whole batch of ammo was flawed – could have gone off any time Farrell pulled the trigger. So, that's the end of the matter.'

Stubbs puffed out air. 'Right, Sir. Thanks very much.'

'I know it was a big day for you, Michael, and I known you're under a lot of pressure, but the safety of your men comes first, always. Understood?'

'Yes, Sir.'

'Good.' Phillips hit Stubbs's upper arm. 'Why don't I meet you in the bar in about twenty minutes. You can buy me a drink.'

'All right, Sir.' Stubbs puffed out his chest again. He stopped and turned. 'Babycham, was it?' he grinned.

Phillips steadied the punch-bag. 'Pint of heavy, if you don't mind,' he said, and resumed his assault on the leather.

'We have heard the evidence,' said the magistrate, and she fixed Donna with a sympathetic eye which did not help much, 'and read all the reports in this matter. We are aware of the attempt the Tuckers have made to improve things for their child, and are glad to see it, but we have decided that significant harm could occur to Macaulay if he were returned home at this point. In the light of this, we make an interim care order in respect of Macaulay Tucker.'

Donna had expected it, but nonetheless gaped. Her head fell into her hands. A whimper seeped through her fingers. Dave was up and behind her, his hands on her shoulders, his lips at her ear. 'It's all right,' he murmured fiercely. 'We'll get him back, love. We'll win. Just you wait. We will win.'

Her right hand rose to grasp his. In this, at least, she realized she needed Dave like she had never needed anyone before.

The truck pulled up high on the down. The lights of Larkhill twinkled way below down at the left. The truck's tailboard banged as it fell, and the CSM was bawling, 'Right! Get fell in! Come on, come on! Jump down! Get cover off! Come on! Hurry up! Go on, move yourselves!'

The soldiers jumped down to this chorus and rapidly formed ranks. The moon was new but bright – a toenail paring above the scudding caul of cloud. The ground temperature was freezing at least, but it was the easterly which made fingers smart and toes feel larger and more demanding than usual. The CSM rapidly set up an easel with a map on it. Forsythe and Stubbs stood at ease on either side of it.

'Right,' the major strolled in front of B Company. 'For those of you who don't know me, I am Major Taylor, your Company Commander. Now, we've got a big show tonight . . .'

'Oh, God,' Joe Farrell muttered, 'Not another Jock. Standards slipping, eh?'

'Shut it!' bawled Paddy. Steam preceded the sound like the explosion before a rifle's crack.

Farrell had misjudged the wind and under-estimated the carrying power of a voice on such a night. 'As Demonstration Battalion, I'd have thought you'd be getting used to us, Gentlemen,' Phillips smiled brightly. 'Now, one of the reasons we're here in Warminster is to make British equipment look as good as it is, so that those watching us will run home and get their governments to spend millions buying it. If you don't look good, your equipment won't. Right! Gather round.' The company jostled closer. Phillips pointed at the Ordnance Survey map mounted on an easel. 'Tonight's exercise. We have to attack a prepared enemy position – here. Four Platoon will attack from here, and Five and Six Platoons from . . . here. All clear?'

'Sir!'

'Right, to your positions, and let's make this smooth and slick, Gentlemen. Thank you.'

NCOs barked. Men climbed tanks and APCs or back into trucks. Forsythe leaped up into his tank with characteristic verve. Engines coughed and groaned into shuddering life. Headlight beams jousted like great lances across the night sky. Taylor breathed deep. He turned to Stubbs. 'Oh, I tell you,' he sighed and smiled, 'after being stuck behind a desk for nigh on two years, it's great to feel the earth under my feet again.'

'Oh, aye,' Stubbs's laugh was a little 'hmph'

coupled with a jerk of the shoulders. 'And what about the frostbite, eh, Sir?'

'That too,' Taylor grinned. He peered down the infra red 'scope. Verey flares were already festooning the valley. 'So, tell me about B Company.'

Stubbs was also watching the fireworks. He hesitated. He said, 'Umm . . .'

'Och, come on, Michael, you're the second in command, aren't you?'

'Yes, Sir, but only as of last week.' He considered. 'They're OK, I reckon. Not a bad bunch of lads, all told.'

'And you and Forsythe?'

'Sir?'

'Oh, come on, Michael. It's my job to know. I heard all about the breech explosion. Now, are you and he going to be able to work together?'

Stubbs pouted but shrugged. 'I can't see why not.'

'Well, I hope you are.' Taylor climbed up into his jeep. 'There's no room for egos here. NCOs can squabble, Michael. It even adds an edge to matters sometimes. Officers, however, present a united front at all times.'

'Yes, Sir,' said Stubbs. It had sounded mild enough, but Stubbs knew – who better? – when he had been on the receiving end of a bollocking.

Down the ranges, things were hotting up, and Dave knew precious little about it. He clung on to the mortar as though to a child. The boom of the big guns was the echo of that bastard Lidgate's voice, the rat-a-tat-tat of the IWs the court stenographer's nimble fingers, recording three lives blown apart.

'De-bus!' someone was screaming, 'Go! Go! Go!', just as there had been roaring in Dave's head for days past – 'No! No! No!' It did not matter. Nothing mattered much. Not now.

Then hands were plucking at him, grasping at his arms, pulling, and Paddy's great ugly face was shoved up close to him, shouting, 'De-bus, Dave! Dave, man! De-bus!'

Dave shook his head, but the clouds would not clear. Forsythe was shouting, 'Tucker! Get a move on!'

'OK, Sir,' Paddy was yelling over his shoulder. 'I'll take care of it!'

A glimmer of hope there. Good old Paddy. He'll take care of it. He's taken care of it so many times before . . .

But Paddy was wrenching the mortar from Dave's grasp, handing it to Joe Farrell, shouting, 'You take that, Joe.'

Dave saw Joe's alarm, heard, 'What, me?'

'You know how to use it!' Paddy barked. 'Go ahead.'

Then Dave found himself lifted bodily, like a child, out on to the turf. On every side, men were advancing, firing. Paddy thrust an IW into Dave's hand. He shouted, 'Get it sorted, Dave! Now!'

Dave blinked stupidly. At his right, Joe sighted with the mortar in the flush of light from the Verey flares.

Paddy was shouting at Joe now. 'We're clear, Joe! Are you ready? Are you ready?' but Joe was wincing, his teeth bared in a terrible grin as his finger tightened . . .

Then – *whoomph*! The tube bucked and flared, and, out there, a tank lit up and rocked like something in a Christmas shop window, sending sparks a hundred feet up.

'Nice one!' Paddy yelled, and swung his arm, 'Go! Go! Go!'

This was a game Dave knew. He had been playing it since he was a little boy – bang-bangs. He was back in the groove dug by years of training, flanking the advancing armour, firing, firing, killing the enemy. And feeling a whole lot better for it.

Marsha had felt that Donna needed an extra shove in the right direction. It was she, therefore, who had summoned the girls for this conflab in a Swindon pub. It was the old team – Donna, Marsha and Nancy – and a new recruit in

Colette, in part because Marsha reckoned that Donna and she would get on, in part because Colette had been looking strangely preoccupied in the past week or two.

For the moment, unsurprisingly, Donna held the floor. 'So, basically, they think I hit him, and they've taken him away and put him in care, and I can't even get to see him until tomorrow, and, er . . .' She bit her lip. It was a strange thing, but, in the past, every story had improved with the retelling, acquiring dramatic or humorous detail as it matured. This one got curter and brisker each time she told it, because each phrase threatened her with collapse and tears.

'Oh, Donna,' Nancy laid a hand on her old friend's, 'I'm so sorry. I'm so sorry.' The faces of the other women said that she spoke for them all.

Donna shrugged and swallowed back the butterfly that fluttered in her throat. 'I keep going into his room, and I just – I just cry . . .'

Marsha was looking to the future. 'So, are you still going to move back in with Dave?'

'Yeah, well, otherwise it would look like it was just a fake, like we didn't mean it. It was my solicitor's bright idea,' she explained to Nancy and Colette. 'He said if I moved back in with Dave, it would present a more stable sort of home to the courts. Huh,' she shrugged. 'Worked a treat, didn't it?'

'So how's he taking it?' asked Nancy, who knew Dave's volatility and his devotion to Macaulay.

'Oh, about the same as me. I mean, afterwards – after the hearing, he kept saying, "Sorry. I'm so sorry," like it was his fault or something.'

'Why?'

'Oh, I dunno. I think because Social Services checked up with the Battalion's family officer, and basically, you know, the message is, if you want a happy, stable family, don't go anywhere near the Tuckers. I mean, OK, I understand that. OK, it was hardly a raging success, but we had more good times than we had bad, and I know – everyone knows – that we love Macaulay more than – more than – anything – else – in the - world!'

'OK,' Nancy soothed. 'Yeah. OK. Shh.'

'Yeah.' Donna drank and smiled as though to an audience of hundreds. 'So, yeah, come on, Nance, how are you set up now, anyway?'

Nancy considered. That hesitation gave her away, thought Marsha. 'OK,' Nancy nodded. 'Yeah, things are OK. Life's sort of settled down. Yeah, it's fine.'

'What is it?' Donna smiled. 'A Mr Military Policeman, is it?'

'No, thank God!' Nancy snorted, then went all coy. 'No, it's a Mr Nick Reynolds, vintage sports car restorer. I got to know him when a tank side-stepped one of his cars. I was handling the enquiry. He told me that either I went out to dinner with him, or he'd sue the Army for millions. You know me. I always put the Army first.'

'Ohh,' said Colette, 'So what's he like?'

'Oh, he's fine,' said Nancy, 'He's not Army, any road.'

Colette's face fell.

'Have you seen Paddy, then?' Donna asked quickly.

'Yeah. Just some Army business.' Nancy looked quickly away.

'Pined away after you left him.'

'Donna . . .' Nancy remonstrated without a whole lot of conviction, 'I did not leave him. We – we agreed to separate.'

'Yeah,' said Donna, with still less conviction. 'Sure.'

'Anyway,' Nancy looked around her for support, 'I mean, he must have found somebody else.'

'Oh, he found quite a few somebody elses.' Donna was not going to let her off the hook. 'Some of them seemed quite serious, but – oh, Nance, he never got over you.'

Nancy looked about her again in search of a different view, but all three girls were nodding sadly in assent, which made her feel just great.

'Not bad, lads,' announced Taylor when at last, muddy and daubed with cam, the men were mustered. 'Not bad at all. De-bus looked a bit ropey, but the rest of it was fine. Good shooting on the anti-tank weapons, too. Who was that?'

'Fusilier Farrell, Sir,' said Forsythe.

Taylor raised an approving eyebrow. 'Well done, Farrell. Didn't think you'd volunteer for that job after the GPMG blew up in your face.'

'*Nor did I,*' thought Joe, but he smiled and said, 'No bother, Sir.'

'Right. That's all, lads. Get back to base. Get your heads down. There'll be plenty of work for you in the morning. Carry on, Sergeant.' He turned to Forsythe as the men were dismissed. 'Mr Forsythe . . .'

'Sir?'

'What exactly was going on, Jeremy?' Taylor asked out of the corner of his mouth. 'Twenty pensioners could have got off a bus quicker.'

Forsythe sighed. 'Yeah. We had some trouble with Tucker, Sir.'

Stubbs stepped in. 'I'm afraid he's been having a bit of domestic trouble, Sir. His kid was taken into care a couple of days ago.'

'Then what was he doing on the exercise, for God's sake?'

'Er, that was down to me, Sir,' Stubbs admitted. He bowed his head as though expecting thunderbolts to rain down on him. 'I decided it'd be best to keep him busy, keep his mind occupied.'

Taylor nodded. 'All right. Yes, I accept that. But if he's got problems, he should be sorting them out, not creating more for us. I want to see Tucker, my office, nine fifteen tomorrow morning.'

Nancy had come in her own car, so Marsha drove Colette back to Warminster. They dropped Donna on the forecourt of Swindon station. They made her promise to summon their aid should she need it in packing up her flat, and Marsha undertook to have a word with 'that useless husband of mine' about married quarters.

It was ten silent minutes later, when the car was nosing out into the wildness of the downs, that Marsha at last asked, 'Come on. Are you all right?'

'Yeah.'

'You just seem a bit . . .' she hit the hub of the steering wheel with the heel of her hand. 'I don't know. You're usually . . .'

'I think Joe's having an affair.'

Marsha took in a sharp breath. This was a complication that she had not anticipated. That Michael might think the worst had been a constant worry over the past two weeks during which she had taken Joe down to the Minster Hotel almost daily, but Colette . . .?

'Sorry?' Marsha tried to inject levity into her tone. 'What on earth makes you think that?'

'Well, you know after his injury, he had a few days off work, right?'

'Yep.'

'And we were meant to do something together, only I couldn't get the time off . . .'

'Yes, I remember.'

'Yeah, well, he took it on himself to disappear down the barracks every two minutes. Well, at least, that's what he tells us. I mean, we've been having some heavy discussions lately, about deep things, you know, Marsh? And I thought it might be a good idea to give him a bit of space, you know? Back off a bit. Let go . . .'

'Yes. So?'

'Well, anyhow, I was tidying up yesterday, and I saw one of his shirts, a smart one, a white one, hanging up . . .'

'And that's bad, is it?'

'Well, no, but I had a look at it, to see if it needed washing, like . . .'

There was a lingering pause. Marsha could stand it no longer. 'Yes,' she prompted, 'and?'

'And that's when I smelt her.' Colette's tone was solemn.

'You *what*?' Marsha nearly exploded.

'Smelt her. Her perfume. On his shirt. Cheap perfume. Oh, yeah, the scent of a very cheap woman, Marsha, very cheap, all over my Joe's shirt.'

Marsha felt like defending her scent, which was *L'Air du Temps* and anything but bloody cheap, thanks, but realized that this might be tactless. 'That doesn't prove anything, Colette,' she said irritably.

'Oh, but it does, Marsha. You don't know Joe like I know him. He hasn't so much as glanced sideways at another woman since he's been with me.'

'Yeah . . .' Marsha could not see the logic here. 'So why do you think he should start now?'

'Well, I don't know,' Colette admitted. 'I mean, when he was in hospital, he did ask for a commitment – a big commitment - you know, name the day sort of thing. And I didn't say yes and I didn't say no either. Maybe he's just given up on me, but I think – I think . . .'

Another pause, this one already in labour.

'Go on,' said Marsha, and she nearly said, 'Push!'

'I think I've pushed him into the arms of another woman.'

'And I think,' said Marsha, 'that you're barking mad. Just you wait, Col. It'll all be all right. Believe me. It'll all be all right . . .'

Chapter 6

'Compassionate leave,' Dave grumbled, 'I said, "what'd I want compassionate bleeding leave for?" Just to go up to Reading and watch Donna cracking up? Great.'

Paddy sighed. Sometimes he despaired of his mate. Sometimes? What sometimes? And they said women let their emotions rule them ... 'Listen, mate ...' he started, but at that moment, a blue Mercedes drew up at the gate, and Paddy had to check the driver's credentials. 'OK,' he told the driver, 'if you'll park over there, then get yourself to the Guardroom. Thanks.'

He straightened and waved the car on. He looked grimly at Dave. Dave knew that look of old. 'Nicky!' Paddy called across to the fusilier in the guard box. 'You take over for a second? Thanks. Great. Now, listen, Dave. Yes, that is exactly what you should be doing, taking bloody compassionate leave and looking after Donna.'

'She doesn't need me. God, she's made that clear often enough.'

'And you believe her?' Paddy muttered a silent prayer. 'God, I don't know.'

'So you reckon I should be up there getting under her feet when she's packing up, and watching our kid in some complete stranger's house just for light relief?' Dave sneered. 'Nope.'

'Come along, Dave,' Paddy urged, 'There must be something you can do.'

Dave was bullish. 'Like what? What, eh? The courts have decided. Mac stays in a foster home till – till I don't know when. So what do you want me to do? We're doing all we can, getting back together again. We watch our steps for however long it takes ... What else is there to do?'

Paddy's lips became a thin straight line. 'I don't know,' he admitted. 'Something. Look ...' he raised his open hand to his forehead. 'Look, you said Mac was taken away because Social Services said he'd been hit, right?'

'Right.' Dave placed his hands on the gatepost and leaned his chin on them.

'They say by Donna. Was it Donna, then?'

'Of course it bloody wasn't Donna.' Dave had to raise his voice as a truck rumbled out through the gates.

'It wasn't Donna. Exactly. Then if it wasn't Donna, who was it? Who? The childminder?'

Dave shrugged. 'I thought so, but Donna doesn't. She says she knows Sandra. She doesn't think she'd do it.'

'Right,' Paddy warmed to his theme, 'and he's been nowhere else?'

'Nope.'

'So, the injury was fairly new, so it has to have been that night when he was at this Sandra's, right? Which means, if Sandra didn't do it, she was covering for someone?'

Dave frowned. 'I don't know. I . . . I don't think so. She lives on her own . . .'

'Yeah, but she's not telling the whole story, is she?' Paddy had the bit between his teeth. He had Dave thinking, and thinking was a darned sight better than moping. 'I mean, I believe Donna, you believe Donna. So it has to be the childminder, but it wasn't the childminder, so it has to be someone at the childminder's. I think you should talk to her, Dave – this Sandra. At least you'll be doing something, and you'll be with Donna.'

Dave studied the traffic sweeping along the road. He said without turning, 'You reckon?'

'I bloody know, man,' growled Paddy. 'Get back there, say thanks a lot, I'll take the leave, and get moving.'

Dave snapped to attention. He saluted. 'Yes, Sah!' he yapped. It was derisive, but at least there now was a glint in his eye.

Paddy was well pleased with himself, then, when Dave passed him a few minutes later with a grin and a wave. The sun was shining, too, just to gild the gingerbread. All in all, it looked like a good day, as days went these days. Days were like babies that way. They started all innocent and lovely.

Then they grew up.

This particular day entered a painful adolescence when Paddy was summoned to Major Taylor's office. He assumed at first that it might be something to do with Dave's problems. For some reason, the world seemed to treat Tucker and Garvey like some sort of double act. When Stan Laurel Tucker got into a fine mess, they consulted Olly Hardy Garvey.

Paddy strolled into the office, then, with an easy gait and a ready smile. He said, 'You wanted to see me, Sir?'

Taylor looked up. He too was smiling. It was a regular love-in, this meeting. 'Yes, Sarn't Garvey, indeed. Have a seat.'

'Thank you, Sir.'

The first inkling that all was not well came when, as soon as Paddy had sat down, Taylor stood up, and, hands linked behind his back, started to stroll. The second inkling came in his statement, 'It's not good news, I'm afraid.'

Paddy braced himself.

'Two sergeants have been returned to the battalion.' Taylor continued his tour of the room.

'Two full sergeants. Which means . . .' He did not need to finish his sentence, but he did so all the same, '. . . that we've now got too many.'

'Yes, Sir,' was the best Paddy could contrive in the way of repartee.

'And I'm afraid that as you have only acting sergeant rank, we can't make you a full sergeant. Which means that you . . . er . . .'

Paddy put him out of his misery. 'Are a corporal again,' he supplied.

'Yes. Yes. I am sorry. Just, there's no arguing with numbers.'

'No, Sir,' said Paddy sadly, just for variety's sake.

'I know this doesn't help much, but I can tell you that, with your record, provided that you keep your nose clean, you should have that third stripe back before the year's out.'

He was right. It didn't help much. Paddy said, 'Thank you, Sir.'

'I am sincerely sorry, Sarn't Garvey.'

Paddy nodded. He stood and crammed on his beret. 'Corporal Garvey,' he said, and smiled.

The sweet, innocent young day's tricky adolescence was prolonged as Paddy left the base to find Nancy walking up the pavement towards him. He had spent eighteen months longing to see Nancy walking up a pavement towards him, but now that it was happening, and he saw the steely look about her, he knew that this was not going to be the slow-motion-embrace sort of reunion.

'I've been trying to get hold of you for two days,' she said, somehow without opening her mouth.

'Yeah. We've been on night exercises.' He hesitated, then thought that he'd have a stab at damage limitation. 'Look, I'm really sorry . . .'

She wasn't going to let him off that easily. 'What did you think you were *doing*, Paddy? Coming round my house like that?'

Paddy shrugged. 'I wanted to see you,' he said simply. 'I got your address out of the phone book. I'm sorry. I should have called you first.'

'Yeah, you should have. Look, Paddy . . .' She drew herself up to her full, not very imposing height. She was decisive. 'It was nice seeing you again. It was very nice. But we split up a long time ago now and things haven't changed.'

Paddy wanted to check this carefully. 'Are you sure?'

'Yeah,' she gulped and nodded. 'Yeah, I am.'

'Right,' he croaked. 'Fine.'

'Right.'

'Was that . . . your boyfriend, then?'

'Yeah.' She was almost whispering now. 'Not that it's . . .'

'Not that it's what?'

They were talking for the sake of talking rather than to convey information. It was a sort of fugue of intimate looks and meaningless words. She realized it, and again pulled herself together. 'Not that it's any of your business, Paddy!' She was suddenly shrill. 'Look, we're over. I've moved on and my life has moved on and you're just not part of it any more. I'm sorry, Paddy.'

'Right,' he said again as she strutted past him, and at least he had the satisfaction of being able to wonder whom she had been arguing with, because it certainly hadn't been him.

Michael Stubbs returned home at half past three. It was a sleepy day back at base because of the night exercises. He wasn't needed there.

He opened the front door to find Marsha, in her coat, picking up the car keys from the hall. She looked up, alarmed. 'Oh,' she said, 'Hi. You're home early.'

'Yeah. That a problem?'

'No . . .' Marsha's expression resembled that of a puzzled puppy. 'No. It's not a problem. I just didn't think you'd be home. I'm just going out.'

'Ah.' Stubbs's tone was laced with danger. Jack-the-Ripper presents *Playschool*. 'How nice. Well, why don't I come with you, then?'

'Oh, Michael, I'm sorry. I'm going to meet friends. It's all arranged.' She cocked her head sympathetically. 'Actually, I'm meeting Colette.'

She had scored a direct hit there. He might have bluffed it out and accompanied her had she said Nancy or even Donna, but Colette was not just beyond the pale, as far as Michael was concerned, she was somewhere off Galway Bay. 'Oh. Fine.' He brushed past her. He picked up some bills from the hall table. 'I'd appreciate it, you know, if, just once in a while, you'd give me a bit of your time. I am your husband, you know.'

'Michael, you know I would have loved to go out with you . . .'

'Yeah.' He glumly split open a brown envelope. 'But you prefer your Donnas and your Colettes – squaddies' women.'

She felt like reminding him that she had once been a squaddie's woman, but that argument could go on for hours. She just said, 'Oh, for God's sake, Michael, it's not like that, and you know it.'

Stubbs studied his gas bill as though it were a love letter. 'Yeah, yeah, yeah . . .' he droned. He walked through into the living room. She heard him sink heavily into a chair.

'This,' thought Marsha as she slid into her car, 'has got to stop. There may be many sins which justify the bust-up of a marriage, but teaching

Joe Farrell to dance must be the silliest, and is certainly the least enjoyable.'

Sandra Quinn opened the door, saw the Tuckers and, almost by reflex, pushed it back in their faces. Dave extended a hand, not to push it open, again, but merely to check it, to give her time to think.

'I've told you,' Sandra's lips worked together as though she were applying lipstick. 'I've told you I've got nothing to say.'

'Please.' Dave held up pacific hands. 'We're not going to cause any trouble, OK? You want us to go, we'll go, but – look, we lost the hearing, right? So Mac's in care. We really need to talk. Please.'

Sandra glared at him like a trapped animal. Her lips still worked, but she pulled the door back and nodded her head towards the living room.

For some reason which Dave did not understand himself, he did not stand back as he would normally have done, but led Donna into the flat. 'Thank you,' he said. He looked around as though he had walked into Fairyland. He noticed a videotape on the coffee table. He picked it up. 'Thomas. . .' He tutted and grinned. 'You've got this as well, hey? He loves it, doesn't he?'

'Yes,' she said abruptly. Her hand trailed along

the back of a chair. It rumpled an antimacassar, but she did not seem to notice. 'What do you want, Mr Tucker?'

Dave stood before another chair. He tweaked his trousers as though to sit, but then just stood there, looking about him. 'It's funny to think of him sitting here, watching telly, all that . . .'

'He's a good boy,' Sandra mumbled.

'Yeah, yeah.' Dave sighed and sat. 'Yeah, he's a good lad.'

Donna did not sit, but sank on to her haunches on the rug where she had last left Macaulay. Her right hand rested in the fur. Whether she adopted this position in order to touch this relic or in some instinctive suppliance, she could not have said herself. 'Look, please, Sandra, can we go over it just once more? Is there any way that he could have fallen and banged his head, or . . .'

Sandra was already shaking her head before the question was complete. She was shaking the words from her skull.

'I mean, I know I didn't hit him,' Donna persisted, 'and I find it hard to believe that you ever would, so is there anything else that could have happened? Is there anyone – I don't know – a visitor, another child – who might be involved?'

'No, no.' Sandra kept up the shaking. 'I told you. We've been through all this before. I told Social Services everything. There's no point . . .

There's nothing more I can say.'

'Please, Sandra,' Donna gazed up at her, 'Please think.'

'I'm sorry . . .' Sandra caught Donna's gaze for a split second. She flinched. 'I wish I could help you, but I can't. Please, will you . . . Will you just go?'

'No!' Donna the Valkyrie was back in the room. It was an Incredible Hulk transformation with which Dave was all too familiar. He thrilled to the power of it, the wildness which pulsed through her. Suddenly her squatting posture was the crouch of a weasel with a rabbit in its sights. 'I've had my kid taken away from me. You'll at least think, Sandra. A child's whole life is at stake here . . .'

Sandra was well out of her range, but still she retreated behind the chair. 'I've said I can't help. I want you to go. Please! You said if I asked you . . . Please, just go!'

Dave jumped to his feet. To Donna's amazement, he was smiling again. 'Right,' he said mildly, 'Sure. We'll go.' He reached down and took Donna's arm. 'Come along, Donna,' he said briskly. 'Right, thanks for looking after Macaulay.'

Donna was so astonished that she suffered herself to be jostled to the door of the flat. Only on the walkway did she recover her self-possession sufficiently to wrench her arm from Dave's grasp. 'Dave!' she protested through fiercely gritted teeth. 'You were right. She was guilty. She was covering for someone! I could have broken her!'

'Aye, for a minute or two, then she'd have retracted it, and meanwhile, you might have made things worse by getting done on an assault charge.'

'I'm not stupid, Dave!' she snarled.

'Never said you were.' Dave escorted her down the iron stairway. 'Listen. You said her old man was Army, didn't you?'

'Yeah? So what?'

'Royal Engineers?'

'Yeah. Yeah, I think so, but he pushed off and left her two, three years back. What's all this about?'

'What this is all about,' Dave explained patiently, 'is a letter down by the settee. Royal Engineers crest on it.'

'So?' Donna's blood, once up, did not rapidly descend. 'So she could have been clearing things out. It could have been from years back.'

'Not,' said Dave sternly, 'with this year's date on it, it couldn't.' He opened the car door and bowed as he ushered her in.

'It doesn't mean a thing, Dave,' Donna insisted as he sank into the driver's seat. 'I told you. She hasn't seen him for years. Leave it. Don't upset yourself.'

Dave raised an eyebrow and started to whistle. He whistled all the way to Donna's flat. Dave could not tolerate impotence. Now, he felt, there was business to be done.

Donna climbed from the car. She looked up at the flat which had been her home. 'All in packing cases now,' she said sadly. 'I had it looking so nice. So. Married quarters ready tomorrow, isn't it?'

'Yeah.' Dave too stepped from the car. He stretched.

'Right,' said Donna in the tones of the condemned man ordering breakfast. 'Tomorrow, I'll hire a van, send the first lot down in the morning. Marsha and Colette said they'd help.'

'Do you want me to . . .?' Dave started.

'No, thanks,' she answered too quickly. 'No. Sorry. Thank you, but I'll manage.'

'Donna . . .' Dave frowned at her over the roof of the car, 'You're not going to change your mind, are you?'

She stared at him long and hard, then a tiny smile momentarily touched her lips. 'No,' she said, swung away and was gone.

Chapter 7

It was over.

Marsha had to confess that her assignations at the Minster Hotel, whilst nerve wracking and frequently painful, had nonetheless proved an engrossing sort of hobby. Joe was an adept and enthusiastic pupil, and had become the darling of the many old women who gathered there at tea time and who, he complained, 'only ever talked about sex'. Marsha had enjoyed the old world ambience of the place. She had even - once Joe had mastered the basics, enjoyed treading a measure again, for Michael's fortes on the dance floor were the night-club shuffle and the embarrassed writhe.

But Colette's suspicions and Michael's sulks had made her mind up, and this evening, she had knocked it on the head for good. Joe had taken it badly at first, but, when he heard that Colette suspected him of having a bit on the side and was afraid of losing him, he was well chuffed.

So now Marsha could return to being an officer's wife. Perhaps, in time, she would learn to play bridge. Perhaps, in time, she would even learn to enjoy it. Somehow, she doubted it.

She drove the car into the garage, switched off the ignition and sat for a moment, smiling in the darkness. She had high hopes for Donna and Dave, for all their current problems, and she was certain that Joe and Colette would get their act together. Was this, then, to be her role? Marriage broker and mender of broken hearts? Mother to the regiment? Dear God, what a dispiriting thought. Oh, it had its compensations, but somehow she did not feel that old. Michael's promotion meant – at least as far as Michael was concerned – that she should suddenly age twenty years and rise – if that was the *mot juste* – ten steps on the social ladder.

Well, she sighed, unfastened the seatbelt and pushed open the door, she was not one to create needless flights, but one way or another, slowly, subtly, she was going to have to correct those assumptions. To judge from Michael's insecurities, he did not seem to be finding the transition that easy, and, if there was one thing that Marsha had learned from foreign postings, it was that there was no figure more absurd, more despised by both contingents, than the Englishman who tried to turn native, to be something that he was not. Michael had earned his promotion by being who he was, not by posturing as a stuffy, braying, port-passing snob. The men would detect the fraud no less than the officers.

So, Marsha concluded, it was her job to calm his insecurities and to build up his confidence in himself. She would start working at it right now.

She let herself in and shed her coat. She called, 'Hi, love!'

'Oi, oi,' Michael called from the living room. 'Have fun?'

She threw her coat down on the chair and dragged her feet as she walked through. 'Oh, it was fine, you know?'

'Good.' Michael was slumped low in the armchair. He sipped beer from a can. He smacked his lips. 'Oh, Colette called by the way.'

Marsha stopped and stood stock still, then wheeled and sank into the chair opposite him. 'Did she?'

'Yup. About an hour ago. She was at home on her own.'

'Ah,' said Marsha.

'Yeah.' Michael was strangely gentle. 'I didn't say anything like, you know, "Isn't Marsha with you, then"?' He sighed very deeply, then leaned forward, forearms on thighs. 'Is there something you wanted to tell me, sweetheart? Because, from where I'm sitting, things are looking a bit bloody odd.'

'Yeah,' she said ruefully. So much for bolstering Michael's confidence. 'Listen, actually there is something I want to tell you, and there's a lot I want to discuss, love, but . . .'

'Go on,' he said, and somehow put together an encouraging smile.

'Well,' she sighed. 'You're not going to like it . . .'

This Supreme Champion Working Bitch of a day was gradually reaching old age and decrepitude. Paddy was eager to hasten its demise. He had already sunk four pints and four double Irish. He did not want to return to his single bed in barracks on his own, but then, neither did he want company unless is was Nancy's, and Nancy would be going to a nice warm double bed with Mr Frank Honest Bloody Nick. A skinful of blessed oblivion therefore seemed a singularly good idea.

'Lager, please,' he told the barman.

'Draught or bottle?'

'Yeah, yeah, that's fine. And a large Bushmills, please.'

'Coming up . . .'

Paddy smiled benevolently about the bar, not because he felt benevolent, but because that was what people who wanted to appear sober generally did. You weren't alone and drunk, not if you were smiling benevolently. Behind him, there was laughter. Paddy turned round on the bar stool, sharing in the jollity.

He frowned, then, and a deep, gravelly sound emerged from him, a sound like something being moved on casters. Mr Frank Honest Bloody Nick was at the centre of the laughing group, and two or three of them were looking straight at Paddy. Oh, they turned away as soon as they caught his glare, but they had been looking at him as they laughed. He was sure of it.

Paddy tossed a tenner on to the bar, picked up the whiskey and knocked it back in one. The heat spread through his limbs. He had to gasp and blink away tears. Again the group behind him cackled. This time, he swung round fast. Yes. They were watching him. Mr Frank Honest Bloody Nick was having a little joke at his expense. Well, he would see about that. He slid from the stool and ambled over. The group fell silent.

'Find me funny, do you?' Paddy challenged the man-who-slept-with-his-wife. And, come to that, how dare a man sleep with his wife? People weren't meant to go round sleeping with people's wives. He'd forgotten that.

'No, not really,' sand the man with a smarmy, superior sort of expression.

'Yeah. Good laugh is it?' Paddy's head drooped. His shoulders came up to meet it. 'Tell all your mates, did you?'

'Look, I think you've had a few too many,' the man advised sagely, aware all the time of his admiring audience, playing to the crowd. 'I think you'd better slow down, pal.

'Well, thanks for the advice, *pal*.' Paddy shoved his face up close and spat out the last word derisively. The man made much of wiping his eye. 'I'll slow down when I want to, thanks.'

'OK,' the man shrugged, 'You do that.'

He made to turn back to his chums, but Paddy checked him with a finger to his sternum. 'Listen. Nancy. She's special. You know that, don't you?'

The man turned his head in an irritable little jerk. 'Uh huh.'

'If you hurt her – if you hurt her, you'll have me to deal with, you hear?'

The man laid a hand on Paddy's shoulder. He said, 'Go home, Paddy. Sober up, mate.'

Paddy made another of those deep growling noises. He seemed to turn away, but then he swung backhand at the smug, smirking, frank, honest, hateful bloody face.

It was a technique which had worked in the past, but on this occasion, perhaps he wasn't quite as quick as he might have been. Perhaps, indeed, he was to conclude later (and not without cringing and blushing), he had telegraphed it a country mile off. The blow never so much as connected. The face just wasn't there any more. What was there, and approaching with unseemly speed, was a fist.

It slammed between Paddy's eyes. Paddy's head jerked back. His already reeling brain rolled freely in his skull. Another fist followed, driving deep beneath Paddy's ribs and forcing the air from his lungs, then another, which caught him on the point of the jaw.

Paddy was flying, backstroke. A table leaped out from somewhere to hit the back of his skull, for good measure, and various chairs scattered noisily out of his way. People were screaming, too, which was strange since it was he who was doing the hurting, and he could not scream at all, though something inside his head was shrieking like a musical saw. He could only lie on his back and taste blood and blink up at a world which was suddenly spinning far, far faster than it was meant to.

Paddy suddenly realized that he might just have made another of his Minor Mistakes.

There were times when old-style gender distinctions were useful. By unanimous tacit consent, this was one of them. Marsha and Colette unpacked the bottles of Jif and the packets of Brillo, filled the store cupboard and hung up the mugs while, downstairs, Paddy and Dave lugged heavy furniture from the hired van and occasionally called upstairs for guidance.

Colette was plucking newspaper from glasses and dropping them into soapy water when she broached the terrible subject. 'Marsha,' she almost whimpered. 'I've found out where Joe goes.'

Marsha was standing on tip-toe to place a jam jar on a top shelf. She paused and remained reaching up like that. Her throat was dry. She had to clear it before speaking. 'Yeah?'

'Yeah. He goes to a hotel in town. I found a receipt in his trouser pocket.'

Marsha exhaled, pushed the jar to the back of the shelf and bent to pick coffee and vinegar from the box. 'Did you ask him about it?'

'Oh, no.' Colette dunked another glass. It bubbled as it sank. 'I couldn't.' Colette snapped on rubber gloves and sank her arms in the suds. 'Oh, it's just worrying me sick, Marsha. I haven't seen him this happy since we first met in Corsica and he used to sneak out of his Foreign Legion base to my hotel room every night. I just can't believe it.' She sniffed, but spoke without rancour. She placed the rinsed glasses on the draining board without even threatening to break them. She was defeated, not angry.

'Listen, just tell me something, Col . . .' Marsha walked back into the centre of the room to heft another cardboard box from the table. 'If you were so against marrying Joe, why did you get engaged to him?'

'I wasn't!' Colette protested. 'I wasn't against marrying him. It was marrying at all – especially into the Army. I think I was scared of what I'd lose.'

'It's not that bad, you know.' Marsha held up a jar full of something green. 'Yuk! What is this?'

Colette shrugged. 'Isn't it? Look at Donna and Dave. Paddy. Even worse, what about Joy Wilton? Come on, Army marriages I've seen are hardly likely to send us sprinting down the aisle, are they?'

'I suppose not. Here. Might as well chuck this unless you think Donna's trying to develop new antibiotics . . .' She slid the mysterious jar down the formica surface. 'But then, there's Michael and me, isn't there?'

'Are you splitting up, then?' asked Colette dully, as though that was what people did.

'No!' Marsha's light laugh spoke of relief. 'No, what I was going to say was that I've had both sides of it, haven't I? I've had a bad marriage and a good one. And if you've a good one, which basically I have, there's nothing better . . . Provided I can survive being an officer's wife, of course. No, but even that . . . It's a boring old cliché, I know, but it's give and take, isn't it? You've got to take. You've got to have the freedom, do your own thing to some extent, look after yourself, all that, but you've got to allow that the Army's important too. It's like a mistress. Let it be a rival, fight it, and it'll win. Give it the space it needs, have a separate life waiting at home, you'll be the mistress he longs to come home to. I reckon there are perhaps ten Army things in a year that I give absolute priority to, and there are about ten things in a year that I make a stand on – weddings, family occasions, disasters at home, anniversaries, you know? The rest is all trivial stuff.' She frowned. She had been counselling herself. She grinned, then. A weight had been lifted. 'Here endeth the sermon,' she said. 'Do you think she uses these plates, or should they go up on the dresser?'

'Dresser,' said Colette. 'Right, so what am I going to do about Joe?'

'Right. I think you've got to find out what he's doing. Confront him. And I'll help you.'

'Yeah,' said Colette dispiritedly. She pulled off the gloves and threw them down on the draining board.

'Oh, come on, Colette. I mean, do you want him back or don't you? You're not going to let this other woman steal him from right under your nose, are you?'

Colette clenched her fists. 'No. No, I'm not. OK, this is the opportunity for me to walk away, but I'm not going to. I do want him back. I'll get him back and all.'

'Good,' Marsha said. 'Attagirl.'

Dave took the rear end of the settee. Paddy took the end inside the van. They eased it out until only two legs rested on the van's floor. Paddy jumped down. He then raised a hand to his head as though to stop its contents from doing their whirling dervish bit.

'Good night, eh?' Dave asked.

'Oh, bloody marvellous,' Paddy groaned. He shouldered the settee. 'Come on.'

Dave lifted his end and walked backward up the garden path. 'Big, was he?' he eyed Paddy's bruised face. 'Lucky punch, I guess?'

'Not really,' Paddy winced at the memory – or at such scraps of memory as remained.

'Come on, Paddy, the suspense is killing me!'

'I had a scrap with Nancy's boyfriend,' Paddy admitted.

Dave closed his eyes for a moment. He tutted, but his grin was one of sheer delight.

'Yeah, I know, I know . . . Go straight back, will you? It's not going to go round the corner. Yeah, right. Smart move. So . . .' He backed into the living room and laid the sofa down. 'How did it go with Cynthia, then?'

'Cynthia? Oh, Sandra! Yeah. Wanted to talk to you about that.' He stood back and pursed his lips. 'There, do you think, or over there?'

'Ah, what's the difference, mate? She's going to move everything whatever you do. So, go on.'

'Yeah, well, she's sticking to her story, but Donna's convinced she's lying, covering for someone, like you said. And there was one thing made me wonder . . .'

'What was that?'

'I saw this letter. Royal Engineers' crest.'

Paddy led him back outside. 'So?'

'Sandra's old man was in the Engineers. I thought he might still be seeing his wife.'

'You're still seeing your wife,' Paddy observed. 'It's not a crime, is it?'

'Yeah, but my wife's not denying that she's seeing me, is she? Gawd, Paddy, I dunno. What a snort or two will do for you. Yesterday, you were the brains – "look into it", "Do something"! Today, look at you. As much vim as a dead sheep. It's obvious, isn't it? If she's covering for anyone, who's it most likely to be? Her husband, right?'

'Yeah.' Paddy leaned on the van. 'Yeah, OK.'

'So I was wondering . . .'

'Go on.'

'Well, Nance is the only person, isn't she? I mean, she could at least check this guy out, find out where he is. And who better to ask her . . .'

'Oh, Jesus,' Paddy moaned.

Chapter 8

Dave sat alone in the flat and fidgeted. He hadn't felt like this since he was sixteen and waiting for Shelagh Gunn to arrive. His parents had been away, and Shelagh was the hottest little number in Whitley Bay with her spikey pink hair and her slashed bondage pants giving glimpses of a body slick and bronzed and full to bursting like a breakfast banger. Then it had been the same. You wanted just enough light not to be too obvious, not too much to banish the mood. You wanted music – not the Clash or the Stranglers, because she'd spend the evening pogoing, but not exactly your dad's *Songs For Swingin' Lovers* either. He'd settled for Blondie. And then there was the wine – one glass poured down the sink so he could casually say, like, 'I'm sure there's some wine chilled somewhere,' and the clothes – oh, God, the agonizing over the clothes – and the Clearasil carefully smudged and blended with his natural skin tones.

That time Shelagh had turned up with two other male friends. They'd drunk all Dave's mum's gin, which had cost him a week's pay.

The following night, she had come to the door unannounced, and him in oily jeans and a tee-shirt. He'd said, 'Er, Shelagh!' by way of a chat-up line. She'd stretched and said, 'You want to do it to me or what?'

All's well that ends well.

Shelagh ended well, come to think of it.

But this was different. He wanted Donna to like the quarters. He wanted her to feel unpres-surised. He wanted it all to be as relaxed and easy and happy as it possibly could be, which, consid-ering that he could not sit in the same place for two seconds without leaping up to plump a cush-ion or wipe imaginary dust off a table, was hardly likely.

The girls had done a great job, he had to con-cede. Everything was sparkling like new. Everything smelt of lavender. The place was warm. Maybe it wasn't quite homely yet, but it would take Donna a few minutes to sort that out, and he had the photographs on the walls, Macaulay's toys all laid out in his room, a vase of flowers on the coffee table . . .

The doorbell shrieked. Dave started, and sud-denly there wasn't a vase of flowers on the table any more. Or rather, there was, but it was lying on its side, spewing water and flowers all over the smoked glass. Dave clenched his fist and exercised a one-footed war dance that would have been approved by a Masai. His curses sounded like pine needles on fire. He shouted, 'Coming!' He reached for the cloth on which the case had been standing, swept the water on to the carpet, crammed the flowers back into a vase and shoved them down behind the settee. There were still water streaks on the glass, so he sat on it, and tobogganed at bit. Then he ran his fingers through his hair and, ever so casually, strolled to the front door.

Donna stood there with a large carrier-bag in one hand, a blue nylon grip in the other. Her shoulders sloped. She walked in without a word. She laid down the two bags. She took in the living room. She said, 'It's nice . . .'

She wandered on to the kitchen. 'Well, it's tidy.'

Dave nodded keenly. 'That was Colette and Marsha. Paddy helped as well. And Joe. It – it's good to see you, Donna.'

Donna placed her hands on either side of the sink and stared out at the trees. 'Oh, God, I don't know. I just walked into this place and I feel like I can't breathe.'

Dave bit his lip. 'Right. Well. It's . . . it's still good to see you. Er – cup of tea?'

'Yeah,' Donna turned and leaned back, arms defensively folded. 'It is clear, isn't it, Dave? I want Macaulay back. That's why I'm here?'

'Yeah,' Dave nodded. 'Yeah, course. We've done upstairs too. There's . . . there's a room for Mac when he comes home. And there's a room for you, you know, that you can use as an office when you're working at home.'

Donna's head jerked towards him. She stared. 'And I'll be sleeping there as well?'

Dave recoiled as though slapped. He still managed to nod. 'Of course,' he said. 'Yeah. Of course.'

Thank God, it was Nancy who came to the door. Her eyes were pale and bright in the lamplight. They were full of mischief. She murmured, 'Well, at least you look worse than he does.'

'Always did.' Paddy gave a little, self-deprecatory shrug. 'Look, Nance, I'm really sorry about that. I'd had a terrible day, and I . . .'

'Paddy, I'm not interested,' she said, but still she did not raise her voice. 'What are you doing here?' She glanced swiftly back over her shoulder.

'I need to talk to you, Nance . . .' Over her shoulder, Paddy saw Reynolds step out into the passage. Paddy raised his head. He said, 'Look, I'm sorry about last night. What can I say? I was – I was pissed and I'm sorry.'

Reynolds moved into the doorway behind Nancy. He said dismissively. 'Fine. Apology accepted.'

125

'Thank you. Nance, listen. I need to talk to you. It's not about me or us. It's about Dave and Donna.'

Nancy jumped as though she'd been woken up suddenly. 'Paddy, please go home.'

'No, I can't. They need your help. Please – please can I come in?'

Reynolds gaped. 'I don't believe this. No you bloody can't mate. Come on, Nance . . .'

But Nancy wasn't listening. Her eyes had locked into Paddy's. She heard only his plea. 'Come on, then.' She pulled open the door. Reynolds seethed.

Nancy led him into the living room. Paddy had time to clock the invitations on the mantel, the dried rushes in the grate, the model cars which gleamed around the room, the heavy-duty stereo system in the corner. He engaged Nancy's gaze once more. 'Dave's got this idea, you see. He thinks that Sandra Quinn's husband might be staying with her, and that maybe he was the one that whacked Macaulay, and she's shielding him. His name's Andy Quinn. He's with the Royal Engineers in Germany. We thought – well, we wondered if you could run a check on him. You've got access to the Army computer, haven't you?'

'Oh, now, wait!' Somewhere in the irrelevant haze behind Nancy, Reynolds was moving and burbling. 'You are pushing your luck, mate. You've got a bloody nerve showing up here, and now you're asking Nancy to break the law.'

'No,' said Nancy irritably. 'It's not against the law.'

'I still don't know why you're getting involved in this, Nancy . . .'

Nancy took a deep breath. 'Because they're f . . .' She stopped, swallowed. 'Will you shut up, Nick?' she snapped. She turned back to Paddy. 'Yeah. OK. I'll do it.'

Paddy sighed deeply. He said, 'Thanks. Like I said, it may be nothing, but thanks . . .' Again he was talking without meaning, letting his eyes do the work. There was a long silence.

'Right, you can go now.' Reynold's voice broke into the reverie.

'Yeah,' said Paddy. He backed away. 'Yeah.'

Reynolds had his arm around Nancy's shoulder again. Nancy stiffened. 'Look, Paddy, I want you to understand,' Reynolds was saying, 'I'm happy with Nancy, and I think she's happy with me. Don't try to break it up, because it won't work. We're OK together, aren't we, Nance?'

Nancy did not answer. She led Paddy back to the front door and held it open for him. 'Well, night, then,' she said softly. Reynolds had not emerged from the living room. 'If I find out anything, I'll let Dave know, right?'

Paddy nodded. He leaned his head against the jamb. Through the narrow crack, he addressed Nancy's left eye. 'I tried to forget you, you know. I tried girls, I tried medals, I tried promotion, drink – everything bar hard drugs, but I still love you.'

She said nothing, but that was all she needed to say.

'Even if you walk down the aisle with Mr Sportscar man and have fifteen babies,' Paddy went on, 'I'll still love you. It's – it's funny. When I'm with someone else, which isn't that often, I have to concentrate real hard so as I don't say your name. It's hard to come to terms with, but you were it for me, Nance. You are it for me. I'm sorry.'

He blinked, sniffed and turned away. Still she stood at the crack in the doorway. Still she said nothing at all.

Chapter 9

Nancy did not stay in that night. Oh, there was no reason to do anything until tomorrow. Mr Andy Quinn would still occupy the same place on the computer's database, and even if she found anything out, there would be nothing that she could do until the day broke.

She just couldn't stay in the house. That was all. Nick was sulking. He knew. People always know, however hard they try to hide from their knowledge. And when he realized that sulking wouldn't work, she knew what would come next. Come on. Make it up. Have a nice evening in. Cosy up on the sofa. Forget about the Army. The past is past.

But the past wasn't past. It stayed with you. You could chuck the albatross over your shoulder so that you didn't have to see it, but you could not stop it stinking. Nancy knew not only what Nick would do, but what she would do in response. She would snap and snarl, compare him with Paddy, cause hurt, push the thing to a conclusion, and she did not want that, not in her present state. She wanted time to think.

She drove to work.

One of the advantages to working for SIB was that the office never closed. Oh, you have to run a gamut of security checks, but, once having established your identity, the run of the place was yours. Nancy let herself into her office, locked the door behind her, switched on the computer and sat in the darkness, staring alternately at the screen and at the window, behind which bare trees bucked and bowed.

The more she thought about the problem, the less there was to think about. Yes, she had always loved Paddy, just as he claimed always to have loved her. He was exasperating, stubborn, gentle, loveable, idiotic. She did not, could not for a moment, blame him for wanting the wife that he had first thought her to be. She too had believed herself to be a dedicated, supportive sort of girl. She too – perhaps because Paddy was such an incorrigible kid – had thought herself to be broody, had wanted his family, but then, she had been brought up thinking so little of herself. Army life had shown her just how much she had to give, and that realization had been intoxicating. Joining the Redcaps had seemed sensible, at least until she decided to settle down. After all, it made use of her qualities, gave her something to do wherever Paddy happened to be posted, brought in extra income. She had not known that she would prove good at it. She had not known that the involvement of the job would make her put family on hold.

No. Paddy had been sold short. No doubt of it. She owed him a huge debt, and would love to be able to pay it, but if she was not yet ready to do so, what was the point of pretending? It would all blow up in their faces again.

And that was what it all came down to. She knew that she would be ready one day, and that that one day might come too late, but was it yet?

Nick did not come into it. She knew that she should be surprised and shocked by this realization. In fact, though quietly embarrassed, she recognized that she had known it all along. With Paddy far away, and only occasionally worrying at the corners of her dreams, Nick had been a charming, amusing, affectionate companion. He had relieved her loneliness, put a spring in her step. She had deluded herself that it was something else, but Paddy had put that delusion to flight, once and for all.

Recognizing that she was getting precisely nowhere, and that this was one of those impossible doldrums which needed a storm of one sort or another before she could even talk about her landfall, she turned to the computer. *Quinn, Andrew Percival, Lance Corporal*, was easily found in the general directory, which directed her in turn to *Royal Engineers*. She called up *Service Record*, which afforded her nothing exciting save a couple of convictions for drink-related offences. And a flashing light referring to INVESTIGATIONS PENDING.

And there is was. A simple, ugly statement of an ugly crime, which should have had Nancy grimacing with disgust.

She was a hard woman, was Sergeant Nancy Thorpe. She grinned broadly. She said, 'Bingo.'

She sat back and glanced at her watch. She had no desire to return home. She would not sleep anyhow. She downloaded the details, including the mug shot. She pulled out the relevant telephone directory to check the address. She fetched the camera from the locked cabinet, returned to the car, and set off for Reading.

Marsha looked resolute as she slammed the car door and led Colette across the car park to the front door of the Minster Hotel. She had to look resolute, first because it was part of her righteously indignant act, and second, because Colette was about as resolute as a bumblebee with Alzheimer's. 'Do you think we should?' had been the initial theme, upon which she had woven elaborate variations such as, 'I won't know what to say,' and, 'It's just not me,' and 'What if she's gorgeous?' and so on. Marsha had remained resolute. Colette's future depended on it. This was no time for faint hearts. Keep that gelatinous upper lip stiff. Up, gals, and at 'em.

Colette uttered one final, 'Oh, dear. You're sure?' before Marsha bustled her into the warm light of the hotel's reception area.

Colette teetered up to the desk. She cast a last imploring glance at Marsha, fumbled in her shoulder bag and pulled out the dog eared but damning receipt. 'Excuse me,' she piped, 'Can you tell me if this receipt is from this hotel?'

The receptionist (now, she was pretty. Could she be the slut/poor exploited wee girl who had filled Colette's tormented fantasies?) smiled like a Rolls Royce radiator and considered the scrap of paper. 'Yes,' she purred. 'That's from our tea room, just in there. Is there a problem?'

Colette gave her a Paddington Bear-style Hard Stare, just to see if the girl would betray her guilt. The girl looked surprised, but Marsha said, 'Thank you so much,' and grasped Colette's hand.

This was it, then. Colette heard the strains of the band becoming louder and louder as the two women neared the bustle and brilliance of the tea room. Just so, she felt, must the bull feel as he goes down that dark tunnel to the thundering arena where his fate is to be sealed. She had thoughts like that, did Colette. Her mam had always told her not to. '*Che sera sera,*' she had always insisted. 'Fancy's for the fancy, my girl.'

Marsha shepherded her up the steps on to the carpeted dais overlooking the room. For a moment, Colette saw what she had thought to see – the pomp and glitter of Prince Charming's ball, somehow invaded by the *dramatis personae* of *Cabaret* – then that fancy subsided and she saw the old women with their support tights, the men with their leather-patched elbows, the paper doileys on paper tablecloths, the age-frosted velvet curtains, and a quintet made up of middle-aged men, for some reason clad in leder-hosen, and a woman in a dirndl.

'There he is,' Marsha was saying.

Colette turned. There he was. There was Joe, brazening it out, beaming as he approached, one hand extended.

'See you!' sang Marsha.

Colette swung round. She caught a glimpse of Marsha's coat as it passed through the door. 'Marsha!' she wailed. She made to follow, but Joe had leaped up the steps and was blocking her way.

'Er, Joe . . .?' she said as he took her hand.

'Care for a dance?'

She pulled herself together. 'No, I don't.' She thrust the receipt at him. 'Two cream teas, eh? Two cream teas? Oh, yeah? With who? Come on. Where is she?'

Joe smiled. She wished that he wouldn't. Not like that. 'She?' he said, 'She's just gone out of the door.'

Colette's head swung round, then her worried eyes again turned to Joe. 'Marsha?'

''Fraid so. Yep. I can lie no longer. She, Marsha, has been teaching me to dance. So, would you like to? Dance, I mean?' He moved closer, took her in his arms.

She tried to push him away, but her heart was not in it. She found herself gently propelled back down the steps. Her eyes were like those of a partisan ping pong spectator. 'Joe . . .? What is going on?'

They were on the floor now. Joe moved in closer, laid his cheek against her. 'I said I was prepared to do anything for you, and anything now includes Rumba, Tango, Latin American, Waltz, and a not very good Paso Doble. I thought we might improve on that today.'

She found her feet automatically taking up the steps of the waltz. She found herself swung around. She also found tears trickling down her cheeks. A lot of involuntary things were happening, and they were all lovely.

'Will you marry me, Colette?' Joe seemed to be having problems with his eyes too. 'I mean, really marry me – find a church, set a date, make a dress, all that?' His little laugh came out more like a sob. 'You better hurry up, you know. See Mrs Briggs over there? She'd dead keen to have me as her fourth husband.'

'Well ...' Colette croaked. She shook her head, despairing of him. He really was a good dancer. 'S'pose ... it keeps you out of strange hotels ... very old women ... gonna have to say yeah, aren't I? Yeah, Joe.' She hugged him. 'Yeah, I will.'

The music went on. The other couples continued to brush past them. But dance was never more than a formal simulation. Joe and Colette had stopped dancing. They were not even simulating any more.

Nancy shuddered as she awoke. She did not for a moment wonder where she was or why she was lying under nothing more than her coat in the driver's seat of the car, nor did she have to worry about the time. She had set her mental alarm clock for half past five. The clock on the dashboard told her that she had overslept by seven minutes.

She glanced around her. The street was empty of human life. There were cars parked all the way along this side of the road, but the other side, where the flats were, was protected by a double yellow line. She had a clear view of Sandra Quinn's window.

According to the textbook, she had parked too close to the target, but she had no back-up, and wanted to be sure that she got a good picture if her hunch was right. She did not want anyone to look out of a window and see a mysterious stranger waking up in a car, but, at the same time, she did not want creaking joints and slow reactions if and when the time came. She again checked the street, and then sat up to perform a few muscle-flexing exercises. She reached down to where she had hidden the camera beneath the passenger seat. She ran a quick check, removed the lens cap and laid the camera on the passenger seat. She covered it with her coat.

She sank down again below the level of the window. She wanted a cigarette, but did not dare. She reached instead for the sandwich and the coffee that she had bought at a garage on the way up last night. The sandwich tasted like a new wallet, the cold coffee like syrup of figs. She watched the flat's window. She watched the outside staircase. She waited.

It was perhaps an hour before the light came on in one of the windows, and even then she did not notice it at once. By then the sky was so light that she had to squint to be sure that it was not a stray reflection. Then someone moved across the light, and she knew.

She glanced about her again. In the rear-view

mirror, she saw a green van lumbering up the gleaming strip of the street. She ducked down until it was past. She was totally exposed, but she saw no alternative. At her left, there was only the open expanse of Palmer Park, and she was damned if she was going to skulk behind the hedges surrounding the block of flats itself, not with such a violent trained soldier for her prey.

She checked, then, that the doors were locked, and wound down the window. And waited.

He came down the staircase fast. He wore a grey sweater, blue jeans, trainers. He carried a gym bag. Nancy registered all this through the telephoto. She had somehow snatched up the camera before she was even aware of it. The motordrive clicked and whirred, clicked and whirred as the man stepped over the grass on to the pavement, looked left and then right, and walked straight across the road towards her.

Nancy dropped the camera between her thighs, sat up straight and turned the key in the ignition. Of course, she was just a secretary – no, a banker, living with her aged mother, heading off to work. The car was cold. It would not start.

A milk float hovered slowly by between the man and Nancy. The man must have side-stepped, for he emerged a good four feet further up the street. Nancy breathed a prayer of thanks to the god or superhero who, in his improbable chariot, had saved her. The man brushed past the back of her car without a glance. He walked on across the park.

Nancy leaned across the passenger seat and quickly wound down the window. Again the camera seemed to consider every shot before clicking. She was getting back views, but he turned his head once to clock a large fluffy dog which suddenly bounded into shot, and, halfway across the path, he veered to his right. Nancy could shoot profiles at leisure.

When at last he was out of view, she again consulted the mug shot. She looked up at the flat. It was once more in darkness. Nancy could nip off, find a bacon sarny and a cup of coffee and be back here easily within half an hour. Let Sandra have her extra sleep. She was going to need it.

'I have no idea why you are even talking to me. In fact, I'm not sure why I let you in.' Sandra Quinn was very grand and shrill. 'I've got nothing to do with the Army.'

'And what about your husband, then?' Nancy asked innocently. 'Corporal Andy Quinn?'

'He's . . . he's my ex-husband.' Sandra pulled her bathrobe tight about her. 'Look, it's very early. I've got to get going. If you'll excuse me . . .'

Nancy did not move from her perch on the table's edge. 'Did you know that he was living with another woman in Germany?'

Sandra gave a sort of squirming shrug. She patted her dishevelled curls. 'As if I care. Like I said, he's my ex. I really don't know or care what he does.'

'And did you perhaps know that he's been absent without leave from his unit in Germany for the past five weeks?'

It was cruel, Nancy thought. No woman should have to lie before she had had a chance to put on some make-up. Sandra's eyes were hunted and desperate. 'So what? He's got nothing to do with me. I told you.'

'Nothing to do with you . . .' Now Nancy moved. She started to stroll very slowly across the room like a TV barrister. 'Oh, I don't think that's quite right, Sandra. You see, I saw him leave this flat just half an hour ago. I have a roll of film which contradicts you.' She did not face Sandra, but looked out across the park. 'Did you know that he went AWOL because he was about to be investigated for abusing his girlfriend's two children?' Now she turned to see the fingers plucking at one another as though to pull off the skin, the lips pulled back in an agonised rictus. She followed up her advantage. 'That child you were looking after – Macaulay

Tucker – that poor little boy now torn from his parents, he hit him, too, didn't he?'

'P-please . . .' Sandra hung a shaking hand out to dry. 'Please will you go?'

'Why are you protecting him, Sandra?' Nancy changed her tune. No turtle-love ever cooed more sweetly and persuasively. 'I mean, what sort of man goes round hitting kids? He's worth-less, isn't he?'

Both women froze. A man's figure had passed by the window. A key now turned in the lock. Through the frosted glass, Nancy saw the dark hair, a broad grey torso, blue jeans . . .

It was Nancy's turn to plead. She turned her eyes to the other woman. She sat.

Andy Quinn strode into the flat.

'Hi!' he called. He slammed the door. 'Got all the way there to find I'd left my bloody wallet . . .'

He entered the room as though playing rugby with invisible opponents. He checked on seeing Nancy. He frowned. He said sharply, 'Who's this?'

Sandra still shook. She looked first at him, then at Nancy. She opened her mouth, but no sound emerged.

'I'm a friend,' said Nancy.

'I said . . .' Quinn walked up to within a foot of his ex-wife, '. . . who is she?'

'She's from the estate.' Sandra gulped. 'She's

asking me about looking after her kids.'

'Yeah? I thought you'd stopped doing that.'

'Oh, yeah, Sandra did tell me that,' Nancy smiled. 'But I thought, you know, seeing as we live so close, I'd try to persuade her . . .'

Quinn said, 'Yeah.' He bounced on his toes and swung his shoulders in a bobbing little pugilist's dance. 'Yeah, why not? I love having kids around. All right, yeah.'

He reached over Nancy's shoulder where she sat. She tried very hard not to seize up. He straightened with the wallet in his hand. 'Yeah,' he said, and bobbed some more. 'Why not.'

A moment later, the door slammed shut again. Nancy's shoulders dropped.

Sandra was more like something punctured. She sagged. Lines appeared in her face where there had been none before. She summoned a dying man's voice from somewhere in her belly. 'What – what did he do to those other kids?'

'He hit them,' Nancy sighed. 'With his hands, with a belt . . . He broke an arm – a four-year-old girl.' She let the words hit home. Sandra sagged further. Her lower jaw had dropped. 'Sandra, did he hit Macaulay Tucker?'

Sandra had raised a hand to her mouth now. Sobs lifted and dropped her shoulders. Her eyes were closed. Still the tears would not come. She shook her head.

'Come on,' Nancy's voice was a harsh twang. 'He's wrecked two families' lives, for God's sake. How many more, Sandra? How many more?'

Sandra panted, then vomited air with a great gutteral roar. Now the tears came, and Nancy was there to hold her, to tell her, 'It's OK, Sandra. It's OK, it's OK, it's OK. It's over now, all over now . . .'

Chapter 10

The families' officer arrived at the Tuckers' just before midday. She drove Donna and Dave to the station, but refused to give them any details, beyond 'It's something to do with new evidence, as far as I can understand it.' Donna grasped Dave's hand at that, and shivered.

The train decanted them at Reading. A taxi took them to the Social Services' offices. It was lunchtime, and Dave assumed that whatever it was would wait until three, or whatever time these people rolled back from their lentilburgers or poodle tartare. Dave, like Donna, was not short on preconceptions.

He was somewhat surprised, therefore, to find that, on announcing their names, they were led immediately through corridors lined with benches and health warning posters to an office marked D.T.RAWNSLEY, and shown in. He was still more surprised to find Nancy standing there, smiling her enigmatic smile.

Dawn Rawnsley stepped forward. 'Mrs Tucker, Mr Tucker, delighted you could make it so quickly. Please come and sit down.'

She returned to her desk. Donna looked from side to side. 'Nancy? What's happening?'

The door opened again. 'Mr Kurtah,' announced a plummy voice, and in bounded the Tuckers' solicitor like a retriever after a ball. Hands were shaken, then Kurtah and Donna were persuaded to sit.

'Right,' Dawn Rawnsley looked vaguely amazed, vaguely amused. 'Now, thanks to information that Sergeant Thorpe has obtained for us, we now have reason – overwhelming reason – to believe that Mrs Quinn's ex-husband was responsible for Macaulay's injuries. Quinn has been arrested and handed over to the military authorities. I would like to say how terribly sorry I am for all the pain that this has caused you, and ask you to believe that Macaulay's welfare really was our first and only concern.'

Dave was punching the air. Nancy was grinning. As for Donna, she had a passionate desire to hug this delightful, sensitive, intelligent woman. Believe her? Of course she believed her. There was such a thing as sisterhood, despite all their apparent differences. But still something was missing in all this.

'What about Macaulay?' she asked.

'We'll have to go back to Court tomorrow to have the care order removed.'

Donna rocked back. 'Tomorrow? Why tomorrow?'

Dawn Rawnsley smiled again. 'I was just going to say that we're very happy for you to take Macaulay immediately . . .'

She was interrupted by Donna's whoop. Mr and Mrs Tucker were for a moment or two indistinguishable. Both were standing. The only difference appeared to be that, while Mr Tucker's feet remained conventionally on the ground, Mrs Tucker's were somewhere around the level of her posterior as she enveloped her husband in an embrace. Soon afterwards, Sergeant Thorpe plunged into the scrum as well.

Dawn Rawnsley cleared her throat. She had to continue doing so for a while before she was heard. 'Sorry,' said Dave, though he could not wipe the grin off his face. He stood to attention. 'Yeah. Sorry.'

'I was just going to say,' Dawn Rawnsley continued, 'that there is one question that the Court is bound to ask you. Will you still be living together?'

Dawn looked quizzically at Dave. Dave shrugged. Donna asked, 'What, will it make a difference, then?'

'I don't think so. I don't know. It may affect their long-term view of Macaulay's welfare.'

Donna paused, but only briefly. 'OK,' she said

146

softly, 'Well, we'll stop then. For the time being, you know; see how it goes, but yeah, OK, we'll stay together.'

'Great.' Dawn Rawnsley radiated a six-foot aura of benevolence.

'Now can we just go and see our kid, please?' Donna was jumping on the spot just like Mac did when there was a present in the offing. 'Please? Can we just go?'

Dawn Rawnsley stood. She pulled her coat from the back of the chair and her bag from the filing-cabinet. She said, 'Let's go.'

It was a weary but contented Nancy who returned home that evening. It was strange how this business had brought home all the good times rather than the bad, the camaraderie which had existed between them all, the deep affection that, she realized, would bind her to Donna and Dave and the rest long, long after her transitory friendships at work and in War-minster pubs were forgotten. It felt good to belong again.

And yet, she knew, belonging had a terrible cost – the absence of privacy, the loss of auton-omy. Yes, she wanted to be with Paddy. Yes, in truth, she wanted a home and a family, but it could not be on the Army's terms, not ever again.

She slouched as she poured herself a drink and

strolled over to the answering machine. She slumped down in an armchair so deep that her feet flew upward. She righted herself and tapped the *Playback* button.

'Hey, Nance . . .' It was Nick. 'Sorry not to see you last night. Er . . .yes, well.. if you're not too tired, come down to the pub, OK? Be there till ten. Bye.'

A beeb. She nestled into the cushions, kicked off her shoes.

Then she spilled her drink.

'*Oh Danny boy, the pipes, the pipes are calling . . .*' sang that voice as it had sung that night, so many years, ago, it seemed, when she had said 'Yes'.

'*From glen to glen, and down the mountainside . . .*' it sang, as at so many parties, on so many nocturnal walks by bays, above the sound of waves in so many seas . . .

'*The summer's gone, and all the roses falling . . .*' it sang, building up to the killer: '*'Tis you, 'tis you, must go and I must bide . . .*'

She would not hear the '*come ye back*' and '*'tis I'll be here*,' not least because she knew from experience that Paddy had pitched it too high and could never hit that top note.

She was up and seething, thrusting her feet into her shoes and hopping to the door as she tried to get the heels on. She snatched up her coat, flung the door open and flung it shut again. She had had enough of this.

Paddy lay sprawled on his truckle bed. He had Ry Cooder on the ghetto-blaster, but he had it turned down low, and he wasn't listening anyhow. He was listening to the wind as it snuffled and woofed at the windows, rattling the panes as it tried to get in, and he was trying to transmit thoughts. He did not know how much there was to this telepathy lark, but certainly he believed that he had in his time received messages on the ether, and it had become a matter of faith to him that he need only close his eyes and think very hard for Nancy, wherever she was, to know a *frisson* and a smile. He was working hard at it tonight.

Of course, the likelihood was that Nancy would simply ring and bawl him out, or that Mr Frank and Honest Sportscar Man would pick up the message and come storming round seeking to close Paddy's other eye. As long as he got to see Nancy again, he did not much care.

The patter of stones on the pane made him jump and smile, but he clasped his hands behind his neck and waited. Again the window rattled, and now he swung his legs from the bed, threw up the lower sash, leaned out and saw Nancy out there in the road, looking, to his eyes, very small.

'Go away!' he called softly. 'We're not married any more!'

Nancy was glaring. She pointed at a point between her feet. 'Get down here now!' she ordered.

He rested his chin on his hands. He slowly smiled. He said, 'No!' then, in response to her continued glare, 'OK, OK . . .'

He sighed deeply, shut the window and padded in his socks to the door, along the corridor and down the stairs. The air outside was blustery and cold and speckled with rain. He swung round the corner of the building, vaulted the low hedge and strode to where Nancy stood. 'Yes?' he demanded.

When it came to defiance, she gave as good as she got. 'What do you mean by leaving messages on my answering machine?'

He gasped and gaped. He pointed to his chest. If he didn't say 'Moi?' it was only because of a natural reserve of which his friends were unaware. 'I didn't leave a message.'

'Don't mess about, Paddy.'

'No, it was your conscience, that's what it was. Like whatsisname's ghost in Scrooge, you know?'

'Paddy . . .' her tone was dangerous. 'I told you to leave me alone.'

'All right,' he nodded, 'I just . . . I dunno. Dave told me what you'd done and I just wanted to thank you.' He flapped his hands. 'You can go now.'

'No!' she yapped, then, 'No, not until you promise not to bother me again.'

'Don't be stupid. I can't promise *that*,' he said as though it were self-evident. 'Tell you what, best thing, see if you can get a transfer to the Falklands. You'll be safe there. I'm allergic to penguins.'

Her lips curled in a smile. 'This is harassment,' she said.

'This is fate.'

Again their eyes had started doing their own independent business. Nancy knew it. She was exasperated with herself. 'Oh, I'm not listening to any of your nonsense,' she growled. She turned away.

'Hey!' Paddy reached gently for her upper arm. 'I'm sorry, Nance. I'm winding you up.' He turned her round to face him. 'It's just Dave and Donna getting Mac again, getting together again, all that. It made me – well, happy. And then, what you did, that was – that was brilliant.'

'It's my job, Paddy.'

'No,' he corrected as though begging her to acknowledge the truth, 'No, Nance. It was friends.'

Nancy's eyes met his again. If she nodded, he saw it there, not in any movement of her head.

She looked away. She looked up at the roofs on the other side of the street. 'I want to ask you a question,' she added. Her voice came out all high and light.

Paddy clapped his hands, puffed air and danced from foot to foot. 'It's bloody cold out here,' he said.

'Tough. You should have put your shoes on.'

'Right, will you wait for me while I get them?'

'No, I bloody won't!' she squealed. 'No, Paddy. Listen. I've been thinking, right, about what you said . . .' She looked down at her feet now, as if they might tell her. 'If – if you really love me so much, why did you let us split up in the first place?'

'Me?' A momentary upsurge of self-righteousness. 'You're the one that wanted to leave.'

'No, Paddy. I wanted to do something with my life. I didn't want to leave.'

He thought about it. It hurt, but he gave it his best shot. 'Yeah,' he said, surprised. 'Yeah, maybe it was me . . . I didn't fight for you, did I? I suppose – it's difficult, you know, Nance, nowadays. If I'd come in on my charger to snatch you away, you'd've told me to sod off and grow up. I'd have given up my job, maybe I'd have ended up with nothing at all, a dosser, and that wouldn't have helped much. No, but you're right. I felt sorry for myself, I felt betrayed. I didn't think it out. Big mistake, eh?' He gave a hollow little laugh. He stepped backward.

Suddenly he doubled up and his face screwed up like a used sweet wrapper. He howled, 'Oh *shit*!' He grasped his right ankle.

Nancy was over him, holding his shoulder. 'What? What is it? Paddy, what is it?'

'Oh, shit,' he grimaced. 'Got glass in my foot . . . it's . . . it's all right, it's all right, Nancy . . .' He pulled himself up with a groan, and hopped. He rested a deal of his weight on Nancy's shoulder. 'Go on,' he winced and waved, 'Go home. I'll be all right.'

'Oh, rubbish,' Nancy snapped. 'Come on. I'm not having you getting blood poisoning and dying on me. Bloody, bloody idiot.'

She stagged a little, but she took his weight and, with one arm about his waist, managed to get him to the barracks' steps. 'Can you make it? One, two, three . . . Oh, God, one, two, three . . . !' She held open the glass doors. 'God,' she murmured as she helped him through the hall, 'if I'm recognized, I'll be crucified.'

'Just – keep – walking . . .' Paddy hissed. 'Close your eyes. Not far now . . .'

Nancy bundled him into the lift. 'Oh, Nance, I'm sorry,' Paddy sighed as the lift whined its way to the second floor.

The doors thudded open. 'Come on,' said

Nancy, and again she puffed as she took his weight. Together like that, they staggered through the door of his room to land in a tangle of limbs on his bed.

Nancy extricated herself and straightened her hair. 'Phew!' she swayed.

'Listen,' Paddy panted, 'I'm sorry about the mess. I only just moved in.'

'Oh, be quiet,' she ordered. She walked to the basin, turned on the tap and soaked a flannel. On a hazard, she squatted down and pulled aside the curtain beneath the basin. She pulled out antiseptic. Behind her, Paddy softly groaned and cursed.

'Right,' Nancy turned. 'Let's have a look at you . . .'

She reached for his sodden sock. She peeled it very, very gently from his calf. She winced as she came to the foot. She lowered her head to examine the damage.

She found a foot. Not a pretty foot, admittedly. Dr Scholl would not be rushing to sign it up in its ads for corn plasters, but it was nonetheless a healthy, pink, unblemished sort of foot. Still worse, its toes were wiggling at her, and its owner was saying, 'Is it better?'

She tried to get up in high dudgeon, but found her arm held. She was giggling when, she was sure, she had meant to be furious, but something had gone wrong between the intention and the deed. 'No! Let me go, Paddy!' she whispered as she tumbled forward on to the bed beside him and felt the warmth and strength of him, the familiar hollows and hillocks that she knew so well.

For all the gentleness of the hands, there was ferocity in the set of the jaw above her as he breathed. 'You wouldn't be here if you didn't want to be. You wouldn't have come round if you didn't want to see me. Would you, darling? You feel like I do . . .'

'No!' she protested, and again an absurd little snigger let her down. 'I thought you were hurt!'

'Only in my heart . . .?' he postured.

She laughed and said, 'Ohhhh!' as she pummelled at his chest. Then he kissed her, and she was still.

'If I get caught here,' she murmured between kisses, 'I'll be busted down . . .' She giggled. 'I'll be court-martialled . . .' He nodded in grave agreement. 'It can't be the same, Paddy . . . We've got to sort it all out . . .'

When she next came up for air, she gave a little squeak, and almost sobbed as she rolled over on top of him, 'Oh, Paddy, Paddy, I've missed you *so* much!'

Little worth reporting was said for a long time thereafter.